Praise for
The Broadway Ballplayers

"Inspirational stories . . ."

—*Los Angeles Times*

"The Nancy Drew of sports . . ."

—*Chicago Sun-Times*

"Sports aren't a pastime—they rule . . . Holohan uses sports to help her characters learn about life. . . . This is not Barbie . . . it's much closer to what you can see in your driveway or local park."

—*Chicago Tribune*

"The stories . . . delve into other issues, including friendship, relationships with parents, gender stereotypes, and social status."

—*Kansas City Star*

"A great series for girls and boys in sports or who want to be in sports!"

—*PMA/Benjamin Franklin Awards*

"It is encouraging to see stories featuring girls who play sports . . . and play sports well. . . . Give this series a try."

—*VOYA*

"Truly exemplifies what sports and life are all about. . . ."

—Dani Tyler, 1996 Olympic Gold Medalist

Books about the Broadway Ballplayers
by Maureen Holohan

ICE COLD
by Molly

Series by MAUREEN HOLOHAN

Aladdin Paperbacks
New York   London   Toronto   Sydney   Singapore

To those who practice
when no one else is watching.

First Aladdin Paperbacks edition April 2002

Text copyright © 1999, 2002 by Maureen Holohan

ALADDIN PAPERBACKS
An imprint of Simon & Schuster
Children's Publishing Division
1230 Avenue of the Americas
New York, NY 10020

The text of this book was set in Concorde BE.
Printed in the United States of America

10 9 8 7 6 5 4 3 2 1

Library of Congress Control Number 2002100144
ISBN: 0-7434-0747-4

Chapter One

You're such a sore loser, Molly," some said as I stomped away.

"It's only a game," others told me.

While I wiped my sweat and tears, a parent or coach always burned me with "Shake it off, kid. You tried your best." Oh, and spare me the "good try" and "you'll get 'em next time." Just give me the letter L for loser and let me do the honor of sticking it on my forehead.

I remember one day when I was at the park playing basketball against Eddie the bully. He pushed my teammates, lied about the score, and argued on every call. After his team won, I screamed "Cheater!" and stormed off the court. On my way home Eddie ran past me and stopped right in front of my house. "Don't you dare step on my property," I warned.

He slurped the saliva in his mouth and tightened his lips. "Don't do it!" I screamed.

With all his might he unloaded the biggest wad of spit on my front lawn. I sprinted over to his house, sucked a mouthful of air, and sprayed spit all over his lawn and my shirt. Eddie grinned devilishly as he walked past me and up his steps (with his jeans hanging off his tight white underwear). I swiped the back of my hand over my mouth, averted my eyes from his gloating, and stomped away.

Losing didn't hurt as badly that afternoon as it did during our first hockey season. I looked in the mirror and saw that L on my forehead. And when I went outside, it felt like somebody else was spitting on my lawn every day.

As I walked down the ramp to the lunchroom, Dawn Miller stopped about ten feet in front of me. She flipped her long, stringy brown hair over her shoulder. Then she crossed her muscular arms and looked down at me. I glared up at her beady brown eyes and refused to break my stride. As I barely brushed her shoulder, Dawn stepped back and yelled, "Look out!"

A few kids turned toward us.

I didn't flinch.

"Stop running into people, Molly!" Dawn continued loudly. A hall monitor turned toward us. Dawn called to her, "Did you see that?" The woman stood up and started walking over to us.

"Give it up, Dawn," I muttered.

"Get a life, *Molly*," she shot back.

Ice Cold by Molly

The way she said Molly made me feel like somebody had cut the oxygen off to my lungs. Somehow the angry shiver that shot up my spine kept me cool, and I continued clear past Dawn. I smiled at the woman, took my place in the lunch line, and told myself to breathe. No Dawn trap for me. Not today. Not like all the years before where she'd sucked me in like a spider flowing down a drain.

When we were in third and fourth grade, Dawn and I had been friends. We used to hang out and talk home runs, crushes, and bad teachers during gym class. But when we hit junior high, the war began. For some reason Dawn didn't want to play on my team. She didn't talk to me except when my back was turned, and then she'd say something mean. I'd face her when the cheap shots became too much, which was always when I was without Wil, Penny, and Rosie, who were my true friends and the Ballplayers from Broadway Avenue.

After my confrontation with Dawn, I thought about how much I missed seeing our oldest friend Angel, who was in high school now. When Dawn raised her voice, Angel patiently talked Dawn out of causing more trouble. I asked Angel once how she kept her cool. She just shook her head and said, "The second you get mad, she wins."

The only time I really got angry was when Dawn picked on people for the clothes they wore and when she drew comparisons to animals. Sometimes she said my pink skin and stocky build made me look like a pig. Fine, maybe I was an active girl who ate more than three square meals a day plus dessert whenever I felt like it.

And maybe I did have fair skin. But calling me an animal that eats slop without his or her hands and makes strange noises was a real kick in the teeth. I thought I had it bad until she told Wil that all her blubber made her look like a whale. After that, I had no choice but to retaliate. Moron, idiot, hook-nosed hockey player. I can't remember my exact words. I felt better until she called my friend Anita Kaplan a skunk at the lunch table. After my carton flew from my hand and chocolate milk smeared across Dawn's white turtleneck, I proudly stood up and headed straight to the principal's office. As I walked down the checked hallway, part of me was still furious at the school bully, but the rest of me was disgusted at myself for ever being friends with a girl like Dawn Miller.

"Don't let her get to you so easily," Angel always reminded me.

"I can't help it!" I shot back.

The worst was when Dawn stole homework and then watched silently as teachers reprimanded innocent kids for not handing in their assignments. The only thing other than bullying people that Dawn seemed to care about was a traveling hockey team she played on. "I'm the best hockey goalie in the city," she always boasted. "Watch me do the splits."

So what if she could press her legs flat against the floor and I couldn't touch my toes? Being so flexible didn't automatically make Dawn any good at hockey or any other sport. The only two people who believed Dawn's claims of being a world-class athlete were her two mismatched sidekicks: Shelly and Nellie. Shelly was tall, full-figured, and spoke with a squeaky voice. Nellie was short, skinny, and had a voice deeper than my dad's. Every day they came to school with the same exact hairstyle. The smell from their hair spray and gel made us want to open the windows in class.

"They're two girls with only one brain," I told my friends one day.

"No, you've got it all wrong, Mo," Wil corrected. "Dawn took the one brain they had, and now they're too dumb to know that they have nothing left."

Wil was right. If Dawn said to pull the fire alarm, Shelly and Nellie would ask what to do after they pulled it. While Dawn tormented kids, Shelly and Nellie stood on the lookout for teachers or adults. They used to whistle or clap different ways. They claimed it was their secret code of communication. I thought it was stupid.

"It's way over your head," Shelly squealed to me one day. "You wouldn't understand."

Dawn was always so predictable. After she failed to rope me into a confrontation during lunch that day, the queen bully then turned to a much easier target. Billy Flanigan sat at a table with a bunch of his friends. He laughed and joked around as he held his peanut-butter-and-jelly sandwich. I knew how much Billy loved peanut-butter-and-jelly because he was my neighbor and I always asked him what his mom made him for lunch. I always asked Billy a bunch of different questions just to get him to stop talking about fire trucks, which were his favorite things in the entire world.

I watched Dawn walk over to Billy's table, and I had a feeling that she was up to no good, like usual. When

Dawn sat down next to his best friend, Paul, Billy's smile turned into a nervous frown. Dawn whispered something to Paul, but he didn't respond. As Dawn leaned in and elbowed him in the side, I clenched my fists. The second Paul reached into his pocket to pull out his money, I sprinted across the room. I weaved through a bunch of kids but arrived too late. Dawn already had the money in her hand.

"Give it back!" I yelled.

"Give what back?" Dawn asked.

"You made Paul give you his money!"

"I asked to borrow it," she said as she turned her palms up in the air. "I'll pay it back."

"No, you won't," I said. "You're stealing!"

"Why don't you mind your own business?" she shot back at me.

"Give the money back."

"Get lost, Molly."

"Not this time."

"I told him not to give his money to her," Billy pleaded as tears filled his eyes. "But he didn't listen to me."

I quickly reached out and grabbed Dawn's hand. I wrapped my hands around her palm and tried to peel her fingers back from her clenched fist. I could feel the edges of the dollar bill, but she wouldn't let go. "Give it back!" I said as we wrestled. "It's not yours, you . . . you . . ."

Dawn pushed me back and we began a shoving match. I felt a bunch of hands tugging my shoulders. "Let her go," my best friend Penny said as she pulled me away. "You're gonna get in trouble!"

6

Wil stepped in and ripped me away from Dawn. "She's not worth your time."

"She stole money from Paul," I reminded her.

"He gave it to me," Dawn claimed. "How's that stealing?"

A few lunch monitors came over, and of course they were too late. I pleaded my case but didn't get very far. All the monitors kept repeating was "Get back to your seats!" Before I walked away, I reached into my pocket, took out my last fifty cents, and tossed it on the table. "If anybody asks you for money, you tell them to check with me first."

Before we left, Penny reached into her pocket and tossed down another fifty cents. I looked up for Dawn and saw her cut into the snack line ahead of a group of angry kids.

"Enough, Mo," Penny said.

"Yeah," Rosie added. "She'll always be like that."

Nothing they said could help me understand Dawn Miller. All I had were angry feelings raging inside of me, and I needed time to cool off. I waited in the lunch line with my friends as they laughed and joked around. After we picked up our trays of food and sat down, they started eating. I stared at Dawn as she sat down across the room. She cackled and high-fived her friends. She winked at any boys who looked her way, thinking she was really cute. I had had enough, all right. It was time for Dawn Miller to pay.

"We need to find a new sport," I told my friends.

"Why?" Wil asked. "We already play everything."

"The basketball season doesn't officially start until

January," I said. "We have a whole month to do something else."

Wilma Rudolph Thomas, who was named after the track star herself, looked up at the ceiling and started to use her brilliant mind. I turned to our best friend, Shantell "Penny" Harris. Penny was Miss Sport of our city. Every kid, boy or girl, wanted to carry her gym shoes. Penny had to be behind me on this one. "What do you say, P.?" I asked.

"I've always wanted to play checkers," she said with a grin.

"A sport is an activity involving physical exertion," Wil said. "Checkers doesn't count."

"It works your brain and your hands," Penny tried to explain.

We all shook our heads and kept thinking. Rosie Jones, the youngest of our group of friends, looked up from beneath her cap with a wide grin.

"How about Ping-Pong?" she asked.

We thanked her for the good laugh.

"I'm serious," Rosie pleaded. "My brother and I play all the time."

"We need a team sport that we've never played before," I said. "Something we all can play together."

"What are you thinking, Molly?" Wil asked.

I grinned. "Hockey."

"We already play hockey," Penny said.

"Not street hockey," I said. "*Ice* hockey."

"What?" Wil gasped. Her blue-rimmed glasses slid down her nose. "You're crazy!"

"Why?" I asked. "What's the big deal?"

"Slippery ice, a tiny puck, a funny-shaped stick," Wil said. "We're talking high degree of difficulty here, Mo."

"So maybe we'll need a little practice," I agreed.

"Who are we going to play against?" Penny asked.

"My dad works with a police officer who coaches at a rink on the East Side," I said. "He'll get us into some games."

"I don't have any skates," Rosie mumbled.

"We'll get you a pair," I said.

Wil and Penny paused and looked at me suspiciously.

"This has to do with Dawn, doesn't it?" Wil asked.

"Not really," I said quietly as my eyes shifted away.

"Yeah, right," Penny said.

"So what if it does?"

"What team is she on?" Penny asked.

"She's with the South Side Sharks," I said. "I think they all play on the same park district and traveling team. We can form a team and play against a bunch of teams."

"Do you think we'll be able to get a game against the Sharks?" Rosie asked.

"I hope so," I said. "I'm sick of hearing Dawn tell us how great she is all the time. Aren't you?"

Everyone agreed, but no one gave me a commitment. I looked across the cafeteria and spotted Jessica Wilson, who happened to be a star figure skater turned hockey player.

"I'll get Jess to play with us," I said. "She's a real hockey player."

"You think she's got time for us phonies?" Wil asked.

"Yeah," I said, ignoring her sarcasm. "She'll play."

"Maybe if we had some time to practice and we had

Jess on our team," Penny said, "it might not be too bad."

As my friends kept talking about the possibilities, my confidence grew. "If I get Jess, do we have a team?"

Wil looked at Penny. Penny turned to Rosie. I smiled at all of them and clasped my hands under my chin.

Wil shook her head and said, "I'll say it one more time for those of you who didn't hear me earlier," Wil said loudly as she looked at me. "Hockey is not an easy sport!"

Just at that moment Eddie Thomas, the king of all bullies at Lincoln School, passed our table. His black-and-gray hockey jersey was tucked into his blue jeans. Eddie stopped and smiled curiously at us.

"You guys are going to try to play hockey?" he asked loudly.

None of us answered.

He threw his head back in laughter. "That'll be a joke!"

"None of us asked for your opinion," I told him.

"I'm Mr. Hockey," he said.

"So no more figure skating?" Wil said.

I burst into laughter and so did a bunch of kids around us. Eddie scowled as he turned to Wil and yelled, "Shut up, Four Eyes!"

I stood up. "Try using your two eyes and see your way out of here."

"You're just jealous," he said. "I know how to play hockey and you don't."

"Like it's that hard to figure out," I said.

Eddie saw our principal coming down the ramp, so he slowly slipped away.

"Eddie may be a jerk," Penny said as he walked away. "But the hockey team he's on is good. I mean, *really good.*"

"I don't care," I said. "We're playing."

So what if Eddie and Dawn had played a little bit more than we played? So what if they were hotshot hockey players on good teams? "I hate traveling teams," I complained. "They always act like they're so much better than everyone else."

"Time out!" Wil said excitedly. "We travel to games by foot, car, or bus for all of our sports. I think the Broadway Ballplayers should be called a traveling team."

"You're right," Rosie agreed.

"It's official then," Wil decided with a proud smile.

Trying to be like Eddie and Dawn did not sound good to me. "I don't want to be called anything else but a team," I said. "The Broadway Ballplayers—that's it."

Then I looked across the room and saw Eddie stop at Dawn's table. Eddie started talking and stared over at us. Dawn then turned toward our table and started to laugh.

"I'm so sick of those two bullies," I said. "I want to bully-bust this school. Just get rid of them all."

"I think we should worry about this hockey deal first," Penny suggested.

"You'd better go talk to Jess before Eddie and Dawn laugh us out of this place," Wil said.

Later in the afternoon Rosie raced down the hallway and stopped right in front of me.

"What's wrong?" I asked.

She looked both ways and waved me closer. I leaned over as she whispered, "I heard from a kid in my class that Jess is playing on Dawn's team."

"What?"

"Jess is playing with Dawn and the Sharks," Rosie repeated. "What are we going to do?"

"It can't be true," I insisted. "Why would Jess play with her?"

Rosie shrugged and said, "Maybe because they're good?"

I scoffed and threw my hands up in the air. Jessica Wilson could not skate with the enemy.

"Don't worry," I assured Rosie. "I'll take care of Jess."

Chapter Two

The bell hummed and I jumped up from my desk. Within seconds the halls of Lincoln School filled with shuffling feet and a roar of voices. As I joined the flow of traffic, I bumped into a few classmates and then was blindsided by others. None of us took the pushing and hurrying too personally. All right, maybe I did sometimes, depending on who bumped me the wrong way and what kind of mood I was in. But that afternoon I had more important things on my mind. I walked up on my toes and then dipped low, peeking through the openings in the crowd. I looked for Jessica's long brown ponytail and red bow.

"Molly!" I heard a voice call out.

I spun around. I breathed a sigh of relief when I spotted Jess waving at me. My nerves tingled as I ran up to the key player who had the power to make or break our team. "Did you get my note?" I asked between breaths.

"Yeah," Jess replied. I waited for a smile. She just stood there staring at the ground.

"Well?" I blurted out. "Are you in or what?"

"There might be a problem," she began.

"No, please don't—"

"Actually, there might be more than one problem," she added.

"Then I have more than one solution," I assured her with a smile.

Jess finally looked at me.

"First, my mother doesn't want me to play on too many teams at once because I might have a chance at making the state traveling team."

Hello? The Ballplayers traveled like every other team. Okay, so the state team was probably a little stronger than ours. "It's all right if you have to miss practice every now and then," I said. "We'll understand."

Jess took a deep breath and rested her hand on her hip. "Are you sure skipping practice will be okay with the rest of the team?"

"Skip as many as you want."

"I still don't know about this."

I lost all patience. "I don't understand why this is such a—"

"Maybe you should hear the second problem before you start telling me what to do."

"Sorry," I said. "Go ahead."

"Dawn asked me to play five minutes before Mary gave me your note," Jess said.

My mouth dropped open. "I can't believe she did that! She must have known I was going to ask you! Well, what did you say?"

"I told her maybe."

"You don't want to play with Dawn," I insisted. "Nobody likes her. She's a bully. You're with us, right?"

"I guess so," Jess mumbled. "But maybe I should think about it some more."

"No, you don't need to think. Your heart is with us."

Jess bit her lip and stared at the ground.

"Don't worry," I assured her. "I'll tell Dawn. She'll understand."

The thought of telling Dawn that the best player in our school was officially on my team and not hers almost lifted me off my feet. But I was the only one smiling.

"Who is playing besides you and the Ballplayers?" she asked.

"Ummm . . . you?"

She rolled her eyes. "Who else?"

"I could get ten players together in a second. Don't sweat it, Jess."

"We'll need more than ten players," she said, "and all of them will have to be able to skate."

"Like I said, no problem."

"Where are we going to practice?" she asked.

"At the rink," I said.

"What rink, Molly?" Jess insisted.

"My dad is working on the details," I said.

No, I hadn't spoken to my dad, but I had faith that he would find a way to help us out. The most important thing was getting Jess to see that teaming up with a group of dedicated athletes for a good cause was the right thing to do.

"How would you like to be our captain?" I said. "You're the best player—you deserve to be our captain!" Flattery started to break her down, so I couldn't let up. "Actually, we already voted and you won," I said. "We need you, Jess."

She huffed. "All right," she said. "But I need to know the details about practice. I've got to work this around my travel-team schedule."

I cringed. The words *travel-team* made me think of Eddie and Dawn, but I didn't say anything. "I'll let you know tomorrow," I said. "Thanks, Captain."

With a huge smile on my face, I bolted down the hallway and stopped in front of Dawn and her open locker.

"Hey, hothead," I said. She spun around. "Did you hear that Jess is playing with us?"

"Keep dreaming, Miss Piggy," Dawn told me. "I just asked her and she said she's playing on my team."

"Wrong!" I said. "She said 'maybe' to you and 'yes' to us. Ha!"

Dawn stepped closer to me. "In about two seconds I'm going to throw you into my locker."

I glared up at her and said, "You're invading my personal space. Would you mind taking a giant step back, please?"

A deep voice boomed, "Molly!" and I jumped two giant steps back. Our school principal clenched his fists as he stormed down the hallway right in my direction. "*I'll* invade your personal space if you don't get your belongings and get out the front door!" Mr. Gordon yelled. "Move it, Miss O'Malley!"

When Dawn chuckled, I wanted to tell her to blow a hockey puck out her ear.

"I mean now!" Mr. Gordon boomed.

I didn't speak until I had packed up my books, slammed my locker, wrapped myself in my coat, and reached the cold air outside. I searched the crowd for my friends and spotted them on the street corner. I ran over to Penny, Rosie, and Wil.

"Where were you?" Penny asked.

"I had to talk to Jess," I replied.

"What did she say?" Wil asked.

"She's in," I replied proudly. "And she agreed to be captain."

"Really?" Rosie said. "I can't believe you talked her into it!"

"She's all gung ho," I added.

"Did you have any problems with Dawn?"

"Dawn who?"

I ran down Broadway Ave. and skipped up the steps of our redbrick house. My brothers, Kevin and Frankie, watched me from the driveway as they paused with snow shovels in their hands. Our little sister, Annie, jogged down the steps, tripped, and fell into the bank of snow on the sidewalk.

"You're going to help us, right?" Kevin asked me.

"I can't," I said. "I've got things to do."

"You never help us do anything around here!" Frankie complained.

My thoughts were interrupted by the soft thud of a snowball against my back. I turned to my little sister. "Oh, like that really hurt."

Annie's hand dug into the wet snow and she gritted her teeth. She wound up, fired, and missed as I darted up the stairs laughing the whole way.

"Nice try!" I yelled.

I didn't have time for this tedious chore and baby-sitting business. Kevin was old enough to supervise, like he normally did when our usual baby-sitter didn't show up. Well, we didn't actually have just one. We had two baby-sitting sisters whom we tortured regularly with practical jokes and strange behavior. Frankie used to lure squirrels and chipmunks into the house just to watch the sisters panic. Another time Frankie locked both of them outside. When I came home and heard what Frankie had done, I felt bad for the sisters, and told my brother that he should grow up. Then I made the mistake of going outside to get the mail. When I came back, the front door was locked. As I banged on the door, screaming and yelling, Frankie watched me from the window with a devilish grin on his face.

We didn't just pick on our baby-sitters. I had a few cherished moments of antagonizing Frankie, too. My little brother hated lobsters, so whenever he really bugged me, I broke out the secret stash of plastic and rubber lobsters I had collected for this purpose. While he wasn't around, I infested his room with the fake creatures. Later, when he walked into his room to go to bed, I'd slam the door behind him and lock him in. He always screamed, cried, and begged me to let him out.

Right before he went berserk, I would back off. If I let the torture go on any further, my mother and father would find out. Then we'd be in serious trouble.

"Come on, Molly!" Kevin pleaded, still holding the snow shovel. "Don't make me tell Mom and Dad you're not helping out."

"I've got an important meeting and some phone calls to make," I said. "I'll make it up to you. I promise."

I ran into the house and grabbed the telephone. I had to speak to my father about my hockey plan before he came home. "Officer O'Malley, please." I waited anxiously until I heard my dad's voice. "Hi, Dad," I said. "Guess what?"

"What?" he replied.

"We're forming an ice hockey team," I said proudly.

"Have you ever played before?"

"Yeah, Dad," I huffed. "We play street hockey all the time."

"It's a lot different on the ice," he said.

"I know, I know," I mumbled.

"Where are you going to play?" he asked.

"That's why I called," I said. "Doesn't Officer Benson have a brother who skates? Or didn't he used to skate? Do you think he can get us some time on a rink? Isn't the rink over on the East Side? When can we start some games?"

"Slow down, honey," he said. "Let's take one thing at a time."

"Okay, fine, Dad."

"Do you realize that it costs money to get time on the ice?"

"Like how much?"

"It's very expensive."

"Oh," I said, and then I paused in disappointment. All of the kids from our street knew that money did not grow on trees. Wil even pointed out one day that "even if it did, we don't have many trees for it to grow on anyway." But I still couldn't give up hope.

"Aren't there any times people can skate for free?" I asked. "Or is there a way we can pay him by sweeping or cleaning or shoveling? I love to shovel."

"I'll find out and call you back," my father replied. "But where are you going to get equipment?"

"I'm going to look for some sales or cheap stuff in the paper," I said. "And there's a used sporting goods store on the East Side." My dad laughed. I didn't understand what was so funny. "Come on, Dad," I said. "We're serious about this."

"All right," he said. "I'll call you back in a minute."

I found the newspaper and some catalogs and started flipping through as I waited by the phone. I had to look twice at the high prices. I couldn't believe how much gear was needed to play hockey: helmets, gloves, mouth guards, jerseys, skates, sticks, and pads for almost every part of your body. I looked at the size of the bags hockey players carried around and was certain that all the shirts, pants, coats, boots, and shoes I owned could have fit inside.

The phone rang and I jumped. I picked it up and smiled when I heard my dad's voice. "It's your lucky day," he said. "A team just dropped out of a league."

My nerves tingled. "When can we start?"

"The only practice times left are early in the morning on Monday, Wednesday, and Friday," he said.

"How early?" I asked.

"Either five or six," he said.

"What?" I gasped.

"That's it if you want it for free," he said. "Your games will be on Sunday mornings at seven. It's a coed league."

"Are the Sharks in the league?" I asked.

"They sure are," he replied. "They play in two leagues from what I hear. That's what a lot of the teams do. Are you sure you're up to this?"

"Yes, Dad. We're sure."

"Hockey is not an easy sport," my father warned again.

"I know," I replied, wondering if he and Wil had been talking sports lately.

"You need to make sure you get the proper equipment and protect yourself."

I didn't listen. All I kept thinking about was how badly I wanted to learn and how much I wanted to show Dawn Miller that the Ballplayers could do anything we wanted to do on hardwood, pavement, dirt, or ice.

"Could you please tell Officer Benson that we'll be there at six o'clock on all three days," I said.

"All right," he said. "But who's going to coach?"

"Can't you?" I asked.

"I wish I could," he said. "But I'm trying to work a lot now so I can help out during basketball season."

"All right," I said. "I'll get somebody else."

I checked the clock as I hung up. I had told the Ballplayers that we needed to have an informal meeting at five P.M. sharp, and they all told me they would report. I knew I had to have my homework done before my mother or father came home, or they'd cancel the meeting the second they walked in the door. I rushed over to the table, dumped my books out of my book bag, and started working. At five P.M. sharp, Wil walked in the front door along with my brothers and sister.

"Wait until you see this," Wil said. She hung her hat and coat on the rack along the wall.

"See what?" I asked.

Wil smiled as she pulled out a rolled-up piece of paper she was hiding behind her back. She said, "You're going to love me for this one."

She strutted over to the table and unrolled her masterpiece. Annie and I looked down at the three-dimensional sketch of a rectangle. "What's that?" Annie asked.

"It's the plan for a rink," Wil said proudly. "I know how much water it needs and how to make sure it's all level. I started working on it during study hall."

I looked at every calculation and angle. "You're amazing," I told Wil. "Billy just jumped on his bike and headed down to the fire department to ask if they'll supply the water," Wil added.

"It's really great, but we already have a rink," I said.

"We do?" she gasped.

I nodded. "Officer Benson got us some time at the rink on the East Side."

Wil sighed and stared down at her sketch. "Billy and I were really looking forward to building this baby," she said. "He's going to take this pretty hard."

"You want me to tell him?" I offered.

"No, I'll tell him," Wil said. "When do we have practice?"

"Monday, Wednesday, and Friday," I said.

"What time?" she asked.

"Early."

"How early?" Wil asked.

I gave Wil a big, phony smile.

"What time, Molly?" she asked again.

"Six," I said.

Wil's eyes bulged.

"It's no big deal," I said with a laugh. "It's better than five and it's free."

"Yeah, sure, Miss Grumpy," she said.

"I'll be fine," I insisted, not really wanting to think about waking up that early.

"Who are we playing against?" Wil asked.

"Mostly park district teams. But Officer Benson said we'd play against some traveling teams, too."

"The Sharks?" she asked.

"Yep," I said proudly.

"When are the games?"

"Sunday mornings at seven," I muttered.

"Oh, great," Wil said as she rolled her eyes. "At least on those days we get to sleep in."

Frankie and Annie sat down next to Wil on the couch and they all started looking through the catalogs. Just as I finished my last homework assignment, Wil started unloading a bunch of hockey trivia on me.

"Who won the gold medal for women's hockey in the 1998 Winter Olympics?"

"That's easy," I said. "The U.S. of A.!"

"That was your warm-up question," she said. "What was the score of the game and who did they beat?"

"I don't know the score," I mumbled.

"The U.S. beat Canada 3–1," Wil said as she smiled proudly. "Now, who was team captain?"

I paused.

"You should really know this one," Wil prodded. "Come on, come on . . ."

I shrugged and then said, "I'm sorry! I don't know, all right?"

"Cammi Granato!" Wil said proudly.

"I knew that."

"If we're going to be good hockey players, we need to know important information about the game."

"What we need right now is equipment, or else we're not going to be hockey players at all," I said.

"Did you know that the great Bobby Orr used old magazines as thigh pads?" Wil asked.

"Really? That's a great idea. What other makeshift equipment can we use?"

"I already talked to Rosie," Wil replied. "She's working on it. So's Angel."

"Will they let Angel play?" I asked.

"I don't think anyone is going to care how old she is," Wil said. "Not when they see how bad we are."

"Can you give us something besides sports trivia and negative energy, please?" I snapped.

"You're telling me that you think you're going to be a regular Cammi Granato or Wayne Gretzky out there? We don't even have skates!"

"I have a pair," I said as I walked over to the closet. I

reached in an old smelly box and pulled out a pair of dirty white skates that had to be a size six. I looked at my big feet and then back at the small skates.

"Go ahead, Cinderella," Wil said. "I'd like to see this."

Penny and Rosie walked through the front door, and I tossed my old skates back in the box. Wil jumped up and blurted out all the news about not having any skates or equipment and then about the early ice time. "I always wanted to roll out of bed and beat my body up in a refrigerator every morning," she said, loving all the attention. "This should be great."

"One minute you're building us a rink, the next you're telling everyone how sorry we're going to be. I don't get you."

"What's there to get? We're beginners playing against traveling teams. You're talking like that doesn't matter."

I looked at Wil and rolled my eyes again. "If you think we're coming in last, then don't play," I said. "That's fine with me."

"What, am I being kicked off the team?"

"I didn't say that," I snapped.

"Let me tell you something, girlfriend," she began. "You need me because you hardly have anyone else."

"I'll find other players," I shot back.

"Enough!" Penny yelled and she looked at me.

"What's the problem, P.?" I asked.

"I have some questions."

"Go ahead."

"Girls or boys league?"

"Both."

"Oh, great!" Wil said.

"Who cares?" I told her. "We play against boys all the time."

"Is checking allowed?" Wil asked.

I nodded.

Wil threw her hands up in the air. "You know how much bigger the boys are in eighth grade," she said. "How's Ro going to hold her own?"

I looked at Rosie and said, "Skate very, very fast."

"Wait a second, Mo," Penny said seriously. "We forgot about one thing."

"What?"

"A coach. We don't know how to play."

The second the words came out of her mouth, my mother walked in the door.

"Hi, girls," she said as she removed her hat and gave us a smile.

"Hi, Ma. I thought you were working."

"I've decided to take a little more time off so I can be home with you kids."

"How about taking a little time out and being the coach of our hockey team?" Wil asked.

I nudged Wil's side with my sharp elbow and gave her a what-are-you-doing look. I didn't want to state publicly that my mother knew absolutely nothing about hockey because then everybody would think I was being a brat and didn't want my mom around. It wasn't personal. When she wasn't yelling at me about cleaning my room or discussing my "lousy attitude," we got along just fine. But being our hockey coach?

"What time is practice?" she asked.

"It's way too early," I insisted. "You need your sleep. You're always so tired from working so much."

"What time is practice?" she asked again.

"Six A.M." I replied.

"Great, I can make it!" my mother said enthusiastically. "When do we start?" My mother reached out her stiff hands and gave my friends hard, stinging high-fives. My friends all laughed. I didn't. My mother went over to the closet and reached for the same old smelly box I had searched earlier. She pulled out a bigger size of cleaner white skates with poofy green balls on the top of the toe.

"You can use these, Molly," she said.

I groaned and my friends laughed.

"They're so cute," Wil said.

"I'm not going for cute," I insisted.

"It's better than nothing," Penny said.

We went through all the equipment in our garage and basement for anything that could work as a pad, glove, or helmet. In the middle of the search I spoke softly to my mom, hoping to talk some sense into her.

"I know you really want to help," I began. "And I want you to coach, but we need someone who knows about hockey. We don't have much experience on the ice."

"I can learn," she said.

"What about being an assistant coach?" I asked.

"Can you find somebody else who can volunteer his or her time at six in the morning?" she asked.

My mind raced again. I looked up and Rosie was staring right at me. "You know anybody?" I asked.

"I can ask my brother," she said. "He had fun coaching us in football. I think he'll do it."

"What a great idea!" I said. "Rico played hockey in high school, didn't he?"

"Yeah," she said. "A little bit. Mostly street hockey, though."

"He must know the basics," I said. "All we need is a little organization and a few drills to get through the season."

"How long is the season, Molly?" Penny asked.

"About four weeks," I said.

My friends all stared at me in shock.

"Four weeks?" Wil gasped.

"It's plenty of time to get ready for the Sharks," I assured them.

"Yeah," Penny said. "If you're playing for eight hours a day."

"Trust me, P. We'll be just fine."

Chapter Three

The next morning I walked up to the kitchen table and reached for the box of cereal. I lifted the box up, shook it, and felt nothing but thin cardboard. Then I turned to my younger brother as he raised his full spoon to his mouth. Frankie's bowl overflowed with our favorite honey cereal. "You're such a hog," I said.

"Mom!" Frankie yelled. "Molly called me a hog."

"Don't start, Molly!" my mother called from the living room.

While I certainly wasn't one to turn down a good meal or snack, Frankie claimed the title as our family's leading garbage disposal. Whenever Frankie stayed overnight at a friend's house, my mother always sent him over with his sleeping bag, pillow, and extra food.

"You're always hogging all the cereal," I said, and then I turned to Annie for support.

"He only gave me a tiny scoop," she said.

"Mom!" I yelled. "Frankie is eating all the cereal again!"

"What am I supposed to do," she asked, "tell him not to eat?"

"Yeah," I told her as I walked over to the toaster. "Skipping a few meals won't hurt him."

"Molly O'Malley!" my mother said firmly as she stormed into the kitchen. "That's enough!"

She stretched the ironing board open in the kitchen and started ironing a few of my father's shirts. My brother Kevin jogged through the kitchen and grabbed a banana. Frankie, Annie, and I sat eating our food and reading the backs of the boxes of cereal. Usually my mother would yell at us for being so rude, but I think that day she appreciated a few minutes of peace and quiet.

"Hey, Molly," Frankie said.

"Hey, Frankie," I replied.

"I heard you're only playing hockey because Eddie plays," Frankie said.

"Who told you that?"

"I'm not telling."

"Mind your own business," I muttered.

"You're always so cranky, Molly," Annie said.

"He's the one who started it."

"You're such a bully," my brother added.

My face felt hot and I stood up out of my chair and said firmly, "I am not a bully!"

"Yes you are!" he said.

The shock of being put in the same category as Eddie and Dawn made my hands shake. "How can you say that?"

"You can be so mean sometimes," my brother said.

"Oh, really?" I shot back. "What about you?"

We bickered back and forth, and my mom started yelling at all of us again. From down the hallway we heard, "That's enough!" from my father. We could tell by his tone that it really was the last "that's enough" before we'd get into real trouble. We all froze in fear for a second, and then brought our quarrels down to a whisper. As Frankie left the kitchen, he grinned and said, "You stink at hockey. Eddie is so much better than you."

I let him chuckle as he walked away. My sweet little brother always enjoyed getting the last laugh. Then I ran into my room and found my secret stash of sea creatures. I pulled out a tiny claw that had fallen off Larry the Lobster. I jogged out by the back door and slipped the claw into Frankie's sneakers. My older brother Kevin peeked around the corner and asked, "What are you doing?"

"Nothing," I said.

"Not the lobster again," Kevin said as he shook his head. "I'm out of here before we all get into trouble."

Kevin grabbed his coat and bag and said goodbye as he left for the high school. I waited patiently for my brother and sister. When I heard my mother's voice, I panicked. For a second I considered how much trouble Larry the Lobster's claw would get me into. I reached down into the shoe but stopped. *She won't see it. She won't care. It's just for a little fun. Leave it in there!*

The Broadway Ballplayers

Frankie and Annie walked into the room, and I grabbed my coat and bag. I watched Frankie reach for his shoe. He picked it up and stuffed his foot inside. He grunted in frustration. Then looked curiously down at his shoe and pulled his foot out. When he reached in and removed the claw, I got ready to make a run for it.

"Ahhhh!" he yelled. He threw the claw on the ground and screamed, "Maaaaaa!"

I sprinted out the door grinning with satisfaction until it creaked open.

"Apologize to your brother!" my mother ordered.

I kept walking.

"Look at me when I'm talking to you!"

I spun around. "He ate all the cereal on purpose!"

"You still want to play hockey?" she asked.

My mother grabbed my brother and forced him on the porch for me to apologize to him. I looked away.

"I'm sorry, Frankie," I blurted out.

"Say it like you mean it," my mother ordered.

I glanced up at my brother's red face and teary eyes. He sniffed as he tried to catch his breath. Nothing made him panic like Larry the Lobster. The moment of glory passed, and I started to feel rotten. "I'm sorry, Frankie," I said sincerely.

Annie, Frankie, and I walked to the bus stop without looking at or talking to one another. I stared far down the street and saw Eddie on his front porch with his two-year-old sister, Suzy. He held her hand and smiled patiently as she walked down the steps in her heavy jacket. When they made it to the end of the stairs, he picked her up and started spinning her around. It was so strange to see Eddie laughing and smiling and talking baby talk. All the other times I heard him cackle and saw him grin like the devil after he did something to hurt someone else. When Suzy's hood slipped off her head, Eddie set her down, bent over, and pulled up the hood.

"Ahh-choo!" Frankie sneezed. Eddie looked right at us. I turned away and pretended not to be watching. After a few seconds I peeked back and watched as Eddie ran his sister up the stairs and took her back inside the house.

I wondered what life was like for Eddie behind those doors. All we heard were the rumors about how his mother had so many boyfriends, and how Eddie's father never came around much. The only time we heard anything was when Eddie's mother was screaming at him. Within seconds of her ranting and raving, Eddie would run out of the house and down to the park. If anyone asked what happened, Eddie would just say angrily, "I hate her."

"Wait for us!" a voice called out.

I turned and smiled at Penny's little brother, Sammy. He jogged up to us with his lunch box and small black book bag. Dressed in her matching blue jeans, shirt, coat, and sneakers, Penny gracefully floated in the air behind him. So did Wil and her little sister, Lou-Lou, but they didn't float. They stumbled with bags loaded with books. Rosie stood alone flipping her baseball in and out of her glove as she waited for us at the bus stop.

"Did you hear about how Shelly and Nellie are all mad at Dawn?" Penny asked.

"Since when?" I asked.

"I guess that whenever Dawn is around her hockey team she pretends she's not even friends with Shelly and Nellie," Penny said.

"You mean, they finally see what's been going on for years?" Wil asked.

"I guess," Penny said.

"No!" Wil said in mock shock.

"I don't buy it," I told them. "When Dawn says jump, they say 'how high' and 'where should I land?'"

"Yeah," Rosie said. "Dawn will probably tell them something really nice, and they'll forget all about what a bad friend she can be."

"I'm not so sure this time," Penny said. "I hear Shelly and Nellie are *really* mad."

I didn't know what to make of the rumors. All I knew is that I couldn't wait to get Dawn on the ice. As we boarded the bus, Eddie and a bunch of kids in the neighborhood started running down the street to catch up. "I'll give you five bucks if you say the windows were foggy and you didn't see 'em coming," Wil said to the bus driver.

The bus driver laughed and said, "I wish I could."

"We wouldn't tell anybody," Penny added with a smile.

Eddie, J. J., Sleepy, and a few other kids sprinted the last hundred yards and sucked air as they piled on the bus.

"Why don't you try being on time for once?" Wil said as they passed us.

"Why don't you try keeping your big mouth shut?" Eddie said.

A few more comments were made, but we all kept a

peaceful distance from one another. As we stepped off the bus, I looked up and saw Jess. She was dressed in her heavy purple-and-black traveling team jacket and matching hat and gloves. "Hey, Captain," Penny said to Jess. "What's up?"

"I just wanted to find out what's going on with the team," Jess replied.

Wil blurted out all the details on practice time, days, and place. "Can you make it?" she asked.

"That's pretty early," she said. "When do we start?"

"Friday morning," I replied.

"How many players do we have on our team?" Jess asked.

"All of five of the Ballplayers."

"Wait," Penny said. "Is Angel playing?"

We had a short conversation about the oldest Ballplayer, Angel, who was a freshman in high school.

"Don't her feet still hurt?" Penny asked.

"I don't know," I said. "Even if they don't, I wonder if they'll still let her in the league because she's in ninth grade."

"It's not like it's going to matter if Angel is too old or not," Wil said. "With or without her, we're still going to stink."

I elbowed Wil in the side. She groaned. I glared at her and then turned to Jess. "She doesn't know what she's talking about," I said. "Angel is really good."

"Who else do we have?" Jess asked.

"Anita, Mary, Jen . . ." I went through a long list of potential hockey players. "Are they all okay with you?" I asked.

"Yeah," Jess said, and her eyes shifted away.

"Is everything all right?" I asked.

"Dawn keeps bugging me about playing on her team," she said.

"What?" Wil gasped.

"Well, if you don't have enough for a team," Jess began, "I might as well play with her."

"We do!" Penny said. "Didn't you hear us?"

We needed action, not talk to prove our point.

"We're having an informal practice tonight at the rink," I blurted out. "We're calling it a captain's practice because you're in charge. Is tonight good for you?"

"What time?" Jess asked.

"Six o'clock," I said. "Can you make it?"

"Yeah," Jess replied. "I think so."

"Don't tell anyone," I added. "Let's just try and keep it for our team only." Jess agreed and she walked away with a smile on her face. "See you later, Captain!" I yelled.

After she left, Penny turned to me and asked, "When did we decide to have a practice tonight?"

I looked at her and said, "We could use the head start."

"Do we all have skates?"

"Are we going to do drills?"

"Are other kids actually going to be out there with us?"

"As long as no one else finds out, we'll be fine," I assured my teammates.

"Why is this such a secret?" Penny asked.

"We don't want everyone to find out where and when we're practicing," I said. "And we don't want anyone to steal our plays."

Penny and Wil started laughing. "Yeah, I'd steal plays

from a team that's never played hockey before."

"Come on," I said. "Stop laughing. I'm trying to be serious and you all think this is so funny. It's not."

"Sorry, Molly," Penny said. "You're right. We'll try not to laugh at you as much as we normally do."

"I don't know if I can make that kind of guarantee, P.," Wil joked.

I ignored them both.

"Just don't let anyone find out about practice because then everyone will know," I said.

We hung outside of school for a few minutes before we had to rush inside to get to class. I heard a few kids laughing over behind the steps, so I looked up. Dawn, Shelly, and Nellie giggled as they packed some snow in their hands and pegged a few kids who couldn't see where they were. Just as I looked up, a ball of snow smashed into Billy Flanigan's face. Dawn laughed and wound up to strike him and his friends again.

As my friends and I hustled over to the scene, Billy's eyes filled with fury. He screamed, clenched his fists, and then stormed over to Dawn. A chill of fear shot through me. All the kids around him stopped and stared in disbelief.

"Leave us alone!" Billy yelled at Dawn.

Dawn laughed at first. When Billy came charging at her with his angry bloodshot eyes and two handfuls of snowballs, it was clear that the situation she had created wasn't funny anymore. She quickly turned to Shelly and Nellie. They took cover behind the garbage cans.

"It wasn't me," Dawn pleaded.

Billy didn't hear her words. He ran straight for Dawn.

For a moment we all stood in shock, speechless at the sight of Billy Flanigan fighting back for the first time in his life. "Come on!" Penny said as she pushed me forward, and then she raced over to Billy.

I didn't move. I just looked around at all of the kids who heard and felt Billy's rage. No longer would he be Dawn's floor mat. There would be no more animal names for his crew. Billy wound up and smacked Dawn with the snowballs. Then he bent down and charged her like a bull. A bull is a good strong animal, by the way, a sheer compliment in my mind.

"Stop!" Penny yelled.

In my opinion, Penny needed to step back and let Billy finish his fury. I looked around, expecting for Shelly and Nellie to storm the scene and bail Dawn out. Both of them stayed behind the garbage cans twirling the ends of their stiff hair around their fingers.

"Let her go, Bill!" Penny pleaded as Billy rammed into Dawn. A mild wrestling match began. "She didn't mean it." Penny tugged on Billy. "Come on, Bill. Let her go!"

Don't let her go, Billy. Keep tugging just for a few more . . .

"Molly! Would you get over here and help me!"

My best friend has a way of covering you with a blanket of guilt, so I jumped in and did the right thing. I grabbed onto Billy's shoulders and said calmly, "Relax, Bill. How about we leave her hair on her head and call it a day?"

Once we got him to let go, Penny and I hung onto Billy for a few minutes as a preventive measure. I could feel him shaking as the tears rolled down his face. Chills shot up my spine. I knew what he felt like and I hated to feel that way. I turned to Dawn. She brushed the snow off and started laughing like it was all a big joke. "You've got to relax, man," she said to Billy. "I was only kidding around."

"Don't you get it?" I screamed. "It's not funny anymore."

As usual, the hallway monitor rushed out the front door about twenty seconds too late. We had already restrained Billy before any damage was done. The crowd quietly cleared. "Doesn't Dawn see what she is doing to other kids?" I asked Penny as we walked away. My best friend did not reply.

I went through the day without running into Dawn again and was glad about it. I tried my best to put her out of my mind and focus on how much fun our first hockey practice would be. All of us alone on the cool ice, having a good time and playing a new game. Ah, I couldn't wait.

"Hey, Molly!" a voice called out at the end of the day. I turned around and looked down at Jeffrey "J. J." Jasper, who happened to be the shortest kid in our class. Both his size and competitive spirit made him a popular kid at school and on Broadway Ave. "Can I play on your hockey team?"

"Who told you I was on a team?" I asked.

"Word gets around," he said.

I huffed in frustration.

"Can I play or what?" he asked.

I stopped for a minute to think of how the Ballplayers and Jess would feel if I invited J. J. to play on our team. J. J. wasn't a marvel on skates or a street hockey wizard, but he took every sport as a personal challenge.

"I've been practicing a lot," he said proudly.

"Sorry, J. I don't think it's going to work."

"I know how to play, Molly."

"Maybe next time."

"I'm serious. Come on!"

I shook my head and smiled at my longtime friend and neighbor. "You'll be the only boy if we let you play," I said. "And I honestly don't think you can handle it."

"Oh, puh-leze, Molly," J. J. said. "I've spent my whole life playing against all you women at the park. Call me Jazmine and consider me just one of the girls."

I laughed for the first time that afternoon. "I can't make any promises, J.," I said. "But I'll put in a good word for you."

"So we have practice tonight?" he asked.

I nodded. "Just a private captain's practice at six o'clock."

"Where?"

"The East Side rink," I replied. "Show up just in case we decide to put you on the team."

"Who's captain?" J. J. asked.

"Jessica Wilson," I replied.

"Really?" J. J. said excitedly. "Jess is the real deal."

"Yeah," I added proudly. "She was going to play on Dawn's team, but she's with us now."

"Cool," J. J. said. "See you at the rink, Mo. Thanks!"

As he strutted down the hallway, I yelled out, "Don't tell anyone!" All the kids in the hallway turned and looked at me.

"I won't," J. J. promised.

Chapter Four

I rolled open the window and let the brisk winter cold hit my face, hoping it would do for me what my mother's cup of coffee did for her. When the car came to a stop, I looked into the lobby of Wil's dark apartment building. A bunch of busy kids buzzed around outside. Wil zipped up the coat of one child and tried shooing them like flies out of the lobby before she came running toward our car. Wil used to say that after seeing so many kids in her building grow up on their own, she was going to write a book about how to be a good parent and make it mandatory reading for the folks in the Uptown Apartments. "Then I'm going to give them a test to see how much they learned," she told us.

"What if they fail?" Penny asked.

"Then they go to jail until they pass."

Seemed like a harsh punishment considering everyone on Broadway Ave. struggled through some tough times. When Wil's mother died a few years back, it was almost as if the sounds of birds' chirping and people's laughing disappeared for a while. Everyone quietly went about their lives, and Wil never spoke about the loss of her mother.

"Wil!" I screamed. "The team bus will leave without you."

Wil tossed her skates over her shoulder, took her time saying good-bye to the kids, turned to me with a mean glare, and clenched her hockey stick. She jogged toward our car and pulled open the door. "Hi, Mrs. O.," she said. "Do you know your daughter has a megaphone for a mouth?"

"If you would have stopped talking," I said, "I wouldn't have had to be so loud."

We stopped and picked up Angel, Penny, and Anita. As they piled in, it took a little bit of organizing to neatly stack the sticks without poking anyone.

"Nobody knows about this private practice, right?" Angel asked.

"Nope," I said. "It's just us."

As we pulled up to the East Side park district, my mom pulled up to the curb and turned to us. "Are you sure you don't want me to stay?" she asked.

Before I answered, I looked up and saw Rosie jump out of her brother's car. "There's Rico and Rosie," I said. "Maybe you should have a coach's meeting in the parking lot."

My mother quickly stepped out of the car, actually

excited that I had given her the green light to do something. My mom occasionally got on my nerves when she wanted to hang out with me and my friends. It took me some time to convince her that I was not a little girl anymore, and that I needed a lot of private time with my friends in order to be happier at home.

"Let me know if you need me for anything," my mom said as she unloaded our sticks from the backseat.

"We'll be fine, Ma," I said.

"Are you sure?"

"Just go talk to Rico," I said.

"Excuse me?" she said.

I reminded myself of the discussion we had on giving adults orders and improving my tone of voice. I huffed and said, "I'm sorry. *Please* talk to Rico."

My friends and I stepped out of the car. As we headed for the rink, Jess burst through the front doors. We all looked up at her wide eyes and waited for her to explain.

"Dawn, Eddie, and a bunch of kids are in there," she said between breaths. "They want to play. Are we ready?"

The Ballplayers and I all looked at one another.

"I knew this was going to happen," Wil said. "I just knew it."

"What a way to start the season," Anita agreed.

I turned to Penny. She looked at me and shrugged. "Let's give it a shot."

I grinned at Jess. She stood straight-faced and said, "We need to play well or they're going to laugh us off the rink."

I looked at Rico and my mother, who were chatting in the parking lot.

"You think we need coaches?" I asked.

"We need everything," Wil said. "Mrs. O. and Rico, come on!"

"What?" my mother called out.

"You're our coach, aren't you?" I yelled.

"You too, Rico!" Rosie added.

They shook their heads and followed in our direction. My mom pulled her hat snug over her red curly hair. Rico strutted alongside her in his black leather jacket and matching gloves.

"We should probably have a quick meeting," Angel suggested.

Jess nodded as Rico and my mother joined us.

"We're scrimmaging tonight," Jess told them.

"On the first night of practice?" my mother asked.

"Yes," Jess said. "Do we have enough equipment?"

We all looked around at our skates and hockey sticks.

"Any helmets?" my mother asked.

"We don't need helmets," I said.

"No playing without helmets," my mother insisted.

I huffed and said, "If we had helmets, we would wear them. But we don't and we have to play."

She shook her head.

"Please, Mom," I pleaded. "We'll be careful."

"I put some helmets in Rico's trunk just in case," Rosie said. "They're old and junky."

We all ran over to the car and pulled out football, boxing, and baseball helmets.

"These are not hockey helmets," Penny said.

"They're all I could find," Rosie said.

"You're dreaming if you think I'm wearing this."

Ice Cold by Molly

I looked at Penny Harris in shock. She could not bail out on us now. I respected the fact that my best friend liked to look cool as much as possible, but now was not the time for style, even if she was a walking fashion catalog.

"Come on, P.," I said. "You can take the blue one to match your blue sweatshirt. It's not so bad." I handed Penny the helmet. She rolled her eyes, reached out, and accepted that she would still be the coolest-looking one of us all.

"Did any of you bring any shoulder pads?" Jess asked. Nobody answered.

"What about thigh pads and chin guards?" she asked.

"We haven't gotten around to that yet," Wil said.

"The goalie has to play with pads," she warned. "Whoever it is can use my stuff."

A few seconds of silence passed as we reached into the trunk and grabbed for the best-looking protection we could find. I got stuck with the bright red boxing helmet.

"No fighting, bruiser," Wil said to me with a laugh.

I turned to my mom as she stared down at me and raised her eyebrows.

"Why are you looking at me like that?" I asked her.

"I didn't say a word," my mother replied.

"I can tell what you're thinking," I muttered.

"You've got to relax, Molly," Wil said. "I was just kidding."

We left the discussion about my short temper on the steps and headed into the rink.

"I don't know about this," Angel said. "Are you sure we're ready?"

"Yes!" I said.

"How many years have you played ice hockey?" Rico asked.

"I started skating when I was four," Jess said. "And I've been playing hockey for about five years."

"Great!" Rico said. "And the rest of you?"

Not a word from the group.

"Do you know any plays?" he asked.

"All I know is that we have to hit the puck without falling on our butts," Wil said. "Is there such a thing as a butt pad?"

Rico shook his head. "Just stay spread out and pay attention," he said. "I'll sub everybody in and out."

We broke from our brief meeting, but the mood grew more serious as Jess led our pack up the stairs. "They've all been talking about us," she told the team.

As we walked into the rink, the music echoed and Penny and Wil started to dance. I searched the crowd. J. J. skated around in a small circle at the opposite end with Eddie and Dawn. He looked at us, grinned, and waved.

"J. J. must have told them," Angel said.

"No," I said. "He's with us."

"What?" Jess said.

"He asked if he could play," I said. "I told him we'd take a vote."

All of my friends turned to me. "All in favor of J. J. being on the team?" I asked as I raised my hand.

Penny said she didn't care. Angel shrugged. Rosie and Anita nodded. Wil wanted to know if he had a day-to-day contract. "You know he gets on my nerves sometimes," she said.

46

I asked Jess for any final comments, and she muttered, "I think we should take whoever we can get."

I announced, "Looks like J. J. is with us."

My eyes stopped on Dawn and Eddie, chatting as they stood on the corner of the ice. After we sat down on the benches and laced up our skates, Eddie skated over to us, and I pretended not to see him. I heard the scraping of his skates as he plowed to a halt. "I heard you wanted to scrimmage," he said.

"We didn't want anything except to come here and practice," Penny replied.

"Why'd you have to come?" I asked.

"It's open skate and we have every right to be here," Eddie said with a grin. He skated off backward and then spun around. "What, are you scared?"

"Five minutes," I said. "You'd better be ready for us!"

Eddie yelled down to Dawn, "Hey, it's on!"

Slowly we started to take the ice. While we all knew the basics of skating, some of us were shakier than others. Wil tripped and stumbled, then caught herself. Anita started laughing and then almost fell over. Penny and Rosie glided across the ice smoothly until Rosie tried to spin around and hit the ice. Penny scooped her up in a hurry. Jess dropped a puck on the ice and started smacking it against the boards.

"How about we just give the puck to Jess and get out of the way?" Wil whispered.

Angel walked up the steps before me and slowly put her feet on the ice. After all of her running in cross-country and in soccer, Angel said her feet felt like they were on fire. I watched her carefully as she stepped onto the rink, hoping the ice would cool them off. She glided off, wincing as she stared down at her feet.

"Are you all right?" I asked.

"Yeah," she said. "It will just take a little getting used to."

Adrenaline rushed through me and I smiled as I put my first skate on the ice and then the second. I clenched my stick and picked up some speed. J. J. skated down to our end and passed the puck to me. I tried to turn around and reach for it. I spun, twisted, lost my breath, regained my balance, sucked in some air, and then completely missed the puck.

"Nice one," I heard Dawn heckle.

My biggest enemy stood at the other end of the rink, but thanks to the way the sounds bounced off the walls, I could hear her every word. I felt like Dawn held a megaphone to her mouth and it was pointed right at my ear.

"She stinks," Dawn said.

I cringed.

J. J. skated up next to me with wide eyes. "Well?" he asked.

"You're in," I said.

"Yes!" he exclaimed.

"As long as you stay off Wil's back, there shouldn't be a problem," I explained.

"Wil's my new best friend," he said.

A whistle blew and I looked up. It blew again. I turned around and saw my mom holding a whistle and waving us over. "Let's go, girls!" she said. "It's time to put on the helmets!"

"Oh, no," Angel said. "Not the helmets."

"What helmets?" J. J. asked.

"Follow me." I sighed in embarrassment and we skated over to our coaches.

"This is one of the disadvantages of having a coach who is a nurse," Wil said as she worked her way over. "Mrs. O. is taking every precaution."

One by one we skated over to the sideline. Jess was the only one who knew how to stop. The rest of us one by one, ran into the wall or knocked each other down like dominoes. *Thump! Thump! Thump!* All the kids on the rink stopped and turned toward us. "It looks like we need to work on putting on the brakes," Rico said.

Jess quickly showed us how to snowplow to a stop. We all took a few seconds to practice as my mother handed out the helmets. All the other kids in the rink started to laugh and giggle. "Don't pay attention to them," Jess said. "They haven't seen us play yet."

Wil raised her eyebrows. "*I* can't wait to see us play," she mumbled.

My mom looked at J. J. and said, "Are you on our team?"

"Yep," he said. "I'm just one of the girls, Mrs. O. Just one of the girls."

Dawn and Eddie called us out to the center of the rink, and we all skated over slowly. Then I guessed the faster I was going, the easier it would be to snowplow to a stop. I started skating and built up some speed. As I grew closer to the group at the center of the ice, I slammed on the brakes. But the blades didn't catch the ice. I spun around, wobbled, and then ran right into Wil.

"Ugh!" she yelled. "Get off of me, Mo!"

The kids on the other team looked at one another and threw their heads back in laughter. I apologized to Wil.

"Don't use me like that again!" she warned.

Eddie skated to the center of the group, and Dawn stood beside him.

"Here are the rules," Eddie said.

"Who says you get to make the rules?" I asked.

"I'm the veteran, you're the rookie," he replied.

"So?" Wil shot back.

"We can check!" he yelled.

I turned to Penny. Checking in hockey was an awful lot like tackling in football. Using your body to block another player is part of the game, but it's not safe without protection. "No," she said. "We don't have any pads on."

"You've got those cool helmets," Dawn said. "What more could you need?"

"Nice try," Penny said. "But no checking."

"How long are we playing for?" Wil asked.

"Thirty minutes," Dawn said. "You think you'll be able to make it that long?"

"While you keep running your mouth off, we're going to be playing," I said.

"Let's go, then," Eddie called out.

Wil decided to be goalie, so she skated back and Anita joined her for defense. Jess lined up across from Eddie for the face-off. Dawn glared at me as she skated off to her spot in the goal at the other end. I watched her the whole way. She put on her helmet, looked at me, and said, "You don't have a chance." Her voice carried loud and clear across the ice.

I watched how fast Eddie was skating and pushed myself to catch up. But I couldn't change direction like he could. One minute I needed to accelerate, the next I needed to go in the complete opposite direction before I crashed and blacked out.

"Slow down, slow down, Molly!" my mother called out. *I can't, Mom, I can't!* All my speed and weight was heading right toward the wall. *Help, Mom. Help!* I watched helplessly, knowing it was only a matter of seconds before *thump!* I hit the wall, folded like a tent, and slid down onto the ice. I jumped back up, hoping Eddie and Dawn had missed seeing my spill.

"You really stink," Dawn said.

"That's it!" I called out as I hurried back into the action. "Pass it over here, P."

I started smacking my stick against the ice. Penny passed it to Jess. "I'm open!" I yelled. I smacked the ice again. Jess brought her stick back and made a perfect pass to me.

"Go, Mo!" I heard my teammates cheer.

With a great rush of confidence, I hustled after the puck determined to show everyone that I knew what I was doing. I stretched my stick out to grab the puck, but I couldn't quite make it in time. When the puck hit the wall, I turned to take the rebound off the boards. I slowed down and focused on turning at the right time. When I turned too sharply, my skates sent me into a wild spin. In a blink my legs kicked out from under me. My arms and stick went up into the air. All my friends' cheers turned into gasps of fear. The lights blurred and I could hear slow voices screaming my name. I held my breath as I did the biggest belly flop of my life. My fall was so jarring that for a split second my world fell painfully silent, but I soon noticed my throbbing rib cage.

"Are you all right?" Penny called out.

"Molly?" J. J. asked. "Talk to us! Are you okay?"

I was afraid to move, unable to believe that I was still alive. When everyone came over to help me up, all I wanted to do was remain on the ground.

"Somebody call the ambulance!" Wil screamed, panicking.

I groaned as I sat up. When I opened my eyes, I saw my mother slipping as she ran across the ice in her boots.

"Sit still!" she commanded. "Don't move!"

I waited for her to come over. She held my head and checked my eyes.

"I'm fine, Mom," I said.

"You're lucky you had that helmet on."

"Did I hit my head?"

"Yes," she said. "You hit it pretty hard."

"It didn't hurt."

"Well, we now know the helmets work," Penny said.

As bad as things were, I couldn't give in.

"Can I play goalie instead?" I asked, thinking that would keep me from falling so hard again.

Wil clicked her tongue and huffed. "Fine, just take my spot without asking!"

"You said you didn't want to play it anymore," Anita reminded her.

While Wil took off her borrowed face mask, shoulder pads, and chest protector, and gave it to me, Dawn skated over and said, "I bet your team doesn't even score on me."

"Get lost, Dawn," I said.

"I can do the splits," she said.

"Wow, really?" I said sarcastically.

"Can you do a split?" she asked. "I don't think so."

Her skates slipped out from under her slowly, and she lowered herself to the ground in a perfect split. A few kids winced in pain.

"That's gotta hurt," J. J. said.

"No, it doesn't," Dawn replied as she turned and faced the other direction. "Goalies are supposed to be able to do this."

I skated back to my spot on goal, wishing by some miracle that I would be able to press my legs parallel to the ground. Then I remembered how hard it was for me even to touch my toes. But nobody in the city could match the way I threw myself around on the basketball court, softball diamond, or football field. I belonged in front of the goal cage.

"Look out, Molly!" Anita screamed, once play started.

All I saw were black blurs flashing in front of my face. Anita, Wil, and J. J. couldn't do anything to stop them. I swatted at the incoming pucks with my glove and stick. One puck sank into the net. Goal number two bounced off Wil's stick and slipped past me. I don't remember goals three through six because so many people were standing in my way and blocking my view. Eddie charged at me on one play and added one more point for his team. "Why don't you try putting a goalie in there?" he heckled.

"Come on, defense!" I screamed. "Can I get a little help?"

With Dawn and Eddie on the opposing team, our

scrimmage during what was supposed to be a private, informal practice, became a very personal nightmare. After every goal, the other team laughed and jeered. All I wanted was for our team to score one goal. Just one. Then Dawn wouldn't have any right to brag about a shutout. Jess and Penny hustled and scraped for a few shots. So did Rosie and J. J. But my wish did not come true. We lost our thirty-minute scrimmage 9–0.

Our coaches called us in as the last whistle blew. Game over. Disaster official. Both teams began to skate off the ice.

"I can't wait to play you in a real game," Dawn said. "Your team is pathetic."

I looked at her and said, "So what if we haven't been playing since we were two. So what? Maybe we just need a little practice."

"Oh, you need a *lot* of practice," Dawn agreed.

I skated off the ice trying my best not to make myself so upset that I would lose my balance and wipe out right in front of the king and queen bully. As I skated, I felt all the aches from my belly flop and the bruises courtesy of the small heavy puck. Angel pulled off her skates and started to massage her feet.

"Anybody have any ice that's not part of the rink around here?" Wil yelled.

Even Penny slumped down on the bench, and Jess wiped the sweat off her forehead. The coaches called our first scrimmage "a great learning experience."

Yeah, right. It's always fun learning how to get crushed.

We sulked and moaned and felt really sorry for ourselves.

"So are you gonna just pack it up and call it quits?" Rico asked.

Nobody answered.

"If that's the kind of attitude you're going to have," my mother said, "then it's not worth even playing."

A moment of silence passed again.

"When do we have practice again?" Penny asked.

"Tomorrow morning at six," Rico replied.

"We'll be there," Penny said.

I stared at my arch rival as she sat untying her skates on the bench in the corner of the rink.

Dawn Miller hadn't seen the last of the Broadway Ballplayers.

Chapter Five

I stood frozen in front of the large metal doors of Lincoln School. Deciding that I could not possibly move forward, I turned around and walked down the steps.

"Where are you going?" Penny asked.

"Let's not go to school today," I said.

Wil clicked her tongue and said, "Where do you think we are going to go?"

"To the park," I replied.

"Yeah, sure," Penny said. "Nobody would find us there."

"It's impossible for any kid from Broadway to skip school," Wil said. "There's nowhere to hide."

"I think I have a fever," I said. "I don't feel right."

Rosie looked at me from beneath her favorite baseball cap. "Why are you acting so weird, Molly?" she asked.

"It's because Dawn Miller is making her sick," Penny said.

"No, she's not!" I said defensively. "You're talking like I'm scared of her. I'm not scared!"

"I didn't say you were scared," my best friend said. "But we all know how much you can't stand her."

"All right, so maybe she's not on my list of favorite people," I said. "Is that a crime?"

"No," Wil said. "But cutting school is."

Wil, Penny, and Rosie abandoned me on the steps and followed a few kids through the front doors. I looked in the parking lot for Dawn Miller but couldn't spot her. She had to be inside. *Why am I letting this get to me? So what if a long time ago we used to be friends? Forget about it!* I skipped up the steps and jogged through the hallways until I caught up with the Ballplayers.

"Mr. G. already asked us where you were," Penny told me.

"I told you that we'd never get away with it," Wil muttered.

"I was just kidding," I said with a smile. "Can't you take a joke?"

I grabbed the handle of my locker and froze. My mouth fell open as I looked closer at the small handwriting just above my lock.

9–0

I blinked twice, hoping the score of last night's scrimmage would disappear.

Wil gasped. "Who did that?" she asked. The anger ran through me so quickly that I couldn't even speak. My eyes began to water.

"Uh-oh," Wil said as she put it all together. "Check this out, P."

Penny looked over my shoulder. "Wait until Mr. G. finds out."

The thought of Dawn Miller even breathing on my locker was enough for me to feel contaminated. The fact that she had the nerve to vandalize my property with a permanent black marker was too much for an emotional girl like myself to handle.

"That's it," I said firmly.

I pushed past my friends and marched down the hallway. With my fists clenched and lips pressed together, I raced up to Dawn Miller. A bunch of boys stood to her right. Shelly and Nellie guarded her left side. When they saw me coming, they stepped into my path. "Move!" I said, pushing past them easily. Then I reached my final destination.

"You think you can write on my locker and get away with it?" I yelled at Dawn.

Dawn pushed her hair behind her ears. "I don't know what you are talking about." Her eyes shifted around the hallway, and she smiled at the crowd of kids who had gathered around us.

"You're such a liar."

Dawn laughed to herself and said, "I still have no idea what you're talking about." Then she turned around and lifted the latch of her locker. She pulled open the door so I could see a big fluorescent sign taped to the inside.

We're #1

"Like my new sign?" she asked.

I looked up to the top shelf and saw the black marker, the weapon she had used to vandalize my locker. I reached up, grabbed it, pulled off the cap, and attacked Dawn's lousy sign.

"Stop it!" Nellie and Shelly yelled.

I grabbed the top of the sign, ripped it off the locker, and tore it in half.

"Molly!" Penny said. "Cut it out!"

"You're in trouble now," Wil said.

I sensed Wil's serious tone and slowly looked up at the person standing next to them. With his arms crossed, Mr. Gordon glared down at me. "In my office, right now," he said firmly.

"Did you see what she did to my locker?"

"I didn't do anything," Dawn said.

"Yeah, you did," I argued. Then I turned back to our principal. "She always lies. Ask anyone."

I looked around at my classmates. They all pretended to look into their lockers for books. "What?" I called out in disbelief. "You were here before we were! One of you must have seen her. Tell him the truth!"

"In my office, now!" Mr. G. repeated loudly.

"Come on, Mr. G.," I pleaded. "She wrote the score of last night's hockey scrimmage on my locker just to rub it in!"

"How do you know it was me?" Dawn asked. "There were other people on our team."

Just as she finished her sentence, Eddie turned the corner, pulled off his winter hat, and rubbed his eyes. Eddie's reputation made him an automatic suspect. His eyes glanced around the hallway. "Why's everybody lookin' at me?" he asked as he brushed the fresh snow off his coat.

"Eddie just got here!" I pointed out. "He didn't do it!"

"Didn't do what?" Eddie asked in confusion.

"It had to be Dawn!" I said.

"This is your last warning, Molly," Mr. Gordon roared. "Get moving, now!"

I threw my hands up in the air and headed down to the office. I could feel the tears build inside of me. *Don't cry, Molly! Don't do it!* There was no way I was giving Dawn Miller or any of her followers the satisfaction of seeing me weep. I counted to ten. By seven I was ready to burst. I pushed open the office door and held on for a few more seconds. "What's wrong?" the secretary asked.

All the anger, hurt, embarrassment and, now, fear of walking into the principal's office hit me like a tidal wave. Mr. Gordon had seen me commit the crime. I had the weapon in my hand and a hallway full of witnesses. The Ballplayers couldn't even stand behind me on this one. I had let Dawn Miller outsmart me. *How could I have been so stupid?* Now she was off the hook and I was in the principal's office crying like a baby.

Stop crying! If I didn't stop my tears before Mr. Gordon stepped into the room, he'd double the punishment for not controlling my emotions. Mr. G. easily distinguished between tears of anger and sadness, and Mr. G. did not like anger. I tried holding my breath, but I burst into a cough after choking on my saliva and tears. Then I started to stare at things around the room and forced myself to think about anything but the predicament I was in. I looked at a basket of fake flowers and thought about my favorite flower. Lilacs. They smelled so nice. I wondered if Dawn Miller even liked flowers. If she liked lilacs, then they wouldn't be my favorite flower anymore, I decided. I looked at a photo of Mr. Gordon's wife and wondered where she worked. Maybe she was a teacher or a principal, too. I hoped she didn't have any Dawn Millers at her school.

The main office door clicked open and slammed shut. Mr. Gordon's picked up the phone and with a deep voice said, "Hold all my calls." I sat upright in my seat, wiped my tears and sniffled. *If I keep myself together, he'll understand. He'll trust me. He'll believe me.*

Mr. Gordon sat down behind his desk. He straightened some papers and cleared his throat. He let a few moments of agonizing silence pass before he leaned back in his chair. "You had no right to do what you did," he began.

"But–" I blurted out.

"No *buts!*" he said. "I want you to accept some responsibility here. It's time to grow up, Molly. Instead of fighting every second with Dawn and Eddie, maybe you should try a different approach."

"I've tried everything," I said.

"How about trying to be friends with them?" he suggested.

My stomach panged with serious pain.

"Well?" he asked. "Do you think you can manage it?"

"I was friends with Dawn a long time ago and she dumped me."

"Try being friends again," he said.

"Why should I?" I asked. "Dawn and Eddie do bad things and you want me to be friends with them?"

"At least try and understand them."

"Understand what?"

"Walk in their shoes for a little while and see what it's like."

I looked away from our principal.

"See things through their eyes," Mr. G. explained.

"What is there to see? It's not like Dawn's a poor kid without a family or money or hope. There are so many kids at our school who have nothing compared to her. Doesn't she live in a nice house over on Fortieth Street?"

Mr. Gordon nodded.

"She has a mom and dad, right?" I asked.

He nodded again. "But that doesn't mean she doesn't have any problems."

"She's mean, Mr. G.," I said.

"Maybe Dawn's had some tough times and it brought out the worst in her," he said. "She acted pretty tough during those times, and now the whole school expects her to be a bully."

"Well, what happened to her?" I asked.

"It's nobody's business but Dawn's," he said. "But it's up to you to find a better way to get along."

"*Me?*" I said. "What about *her?*"

He shook his head in disappointment. "Try not to be so

62

hard on some people, and maybe they won't be so hard on everyone else. See things through their eyes. Walk in their shoes. They have feelings, too."

"Feelings? What about Billy and Paul and Anita? Dawn walks all over their feelings. What about when Dawn and Eddie call Wil fat? They could try walking in our shoes for once."

"Maybe Dawn and Eddie will if you try to meet them halfway," he said.

This was stupid and hopeless. A total waste of time. I stared at the clock on the wall and hoped I would be released in time for gym class.

"As a punishment for your bad behavior. . .," Mr. G. began. I looked up in shock. A punishment? We'd been talking about this like adults. I was listening. Wasn't that enough?

"One detention after school today," he said.

"What?" I gasped. "What did I do?"

"First, you did not respect other people's property," he said. I started to cry again. "Second, you disrespected me when I asked you to go to my office."

"What about Dawn?" I said as I wiped my tears.

"If there was a problem, you should have come to me first," he said.

"She's the one who's lying," I mumbled. "And I get all the blame because she was sneakier than I was. Oh, that's fair."

Mr. Gordon ignored my pleas and ended our meeting with the details of my punishment. "For the entire hour of detention you will be scrubbing any writing off the walls in the girls' bathrooms."

My jaw dropped.

"And one more thing," he said as he stood up and ushered me out the door. "I'm calling your mother and father."

My heart stopped. "Come on, Mr. G.," I said. "I promise not to start any more trouble with Dawn. I promise."

"See you after school," he said.

I left the main office and walked down the hallway in a daze. I didn't think about Dawn Miller or Eddie Thompson. I didn't think about scrubbing the disgusting bathroom walls. My mind raced, wondering whom Mr. G. would talk to first: my mother or my father.

I spent the majority of my one-hour detention after school removing two big letter *D*s off the inside of two separate bathroom doors. Of course the D stood for Dawn. I mentioned this to Mr. Gordon as he zipped down the hallway, but he kept walking and told me to "keep scrubbing." Other girls who were still in the building for after-school activities stared down at me and then looked away without a word. I imagined what they'd be saying about me: *"Look at Molly. She's in detention. What a loser."*

After the hour I reported to Mr. Gordon and he released me.

"Tomorrow is a new day," he said. "See you then."

Mr. G. reminded me again about the walking-in-a-bully's-shoes thing and I thought about it as I dragged my boots through the snow and slush. I wondered if Mr. G. had tried to step into my shoes and feel how angry I was at Dawn. If he had, then he probably would have felt sorry for me, instead of punishing me and giving me the walk-in-shoes lecture. I wondered if my dad tried to walk in the shoes of criminals and crooks. *If we all took pity on people, nobody would go to jail. No one would be at fault. Why didn't I think of this earlier? I'll tell Mr. G. tomorrow. He'll apologize and say I'm right. Then he'll go find Dawn and make her scrub the walls of all the really disgusting boys' bathrooms.*

I pushed open the back door and Annie ran up to me. "You're in trouble!" she said.

"Mind your own business," I mumbled.

"Mom called and said you can't go to hockey practice in the morning," Annie said.

"How do you know?" I said.

"I heard Dad on the phone with Mom," she said and then ran out of the back room.

Being sent to the principal's office wasn't unusual. Cleaning bathrooms stunk, but I survived. Yet the thought of missing our first hockey practice when it was my idea to start the team in the first place was so cruel, so wrong.

"Molly," I heard my dad's voice call. "I'd like to talk to you."

I dragged my bag of books behind me as I walked into the kitchen and took a seat at the table.

"Would you please explain what happened in school today?" he asked.

"Dawn started it."

My dad angrily tossed the towel in the sink and shook his head. He glared at me and I looked away. I decided to let my father do the talking.

"Mr. Gordon and I talked about responsibility today,"

my father said, his voice rising. My sister peeked from around the corner.

"In your room, Annie!" my father shouted. She disappeared in a hurry. Then my father turned back to me and asked, "When are you going to accept some responsibility, Molly?"

I wasn't sure if I was supposed to answer, so I just sat there.

"When?" he repeated.

"Dawn treats other people like dirt," I said. "And I have to take the blame?"

"No," he replied. "Just think before you act for once and don't worry about anyone else."

I shook my head and began to cry. My father was telling me to not worry about anyone else. Mr. Gordon was telling me to walk in somebody else's shoes. They had no idea what it was like to be within fifty feet of bullies like Eddie and Dawn every day. Just when I thought it couldn't get any worse, my dad dropped the bomb. "No hockey practice for you in the morning," he said.

"Please Dad!" I blurted out.

"If you have any other problems directly related to Dawn Miller," my father warned, "you will be taken off the hockey team for good."

He paused for a moment and I stared at my heavy bag of homework. "Now go wash your hands and help me set the table," he added.

I went into the bathroom and looked at my red face and eyes. I wet a washcloth and tried to wash all the tears away. *Why can't I be more like Penny and Rosie? They never cry.* After about thirty seconds I remembered how many times I had tried washing the redness away and it never worked. Dawn Miller turned me into this mess. I didn't care what anyone said. She still had to pay.

Later that night I lay in bed and tried to think of at least twenty-five different comebacks I could use the next time Dawn made fun of me or picked on anyone else. Instead of screaming or crying, I'd wear a big smile and laugh hysterically and treat her like one big, walking joke.

Then I jumped up from my bed and sat on my floor. I stretched my legs out one at a time, and then tried to lower myself into a perfect split. My right knee bent and I felt the painful stretching of my leg muscles. I grunted, groaned, and kept pressing down. My legs wouldn't go any farther. I kept trying.

"What are you doing?" my father whispered as he pushed open my door.

I jumped up and ducked back under the covers of my bed. "Nothin'," I said. My legs still ached as I held my breath.

"Good night, Molly," my father said.

I woke up the next morning at five-thirty A.M. and thought about what the Ballplayers would be saying about me for missing the first practice. I heard my mother leave for the rink and tried to fall back asleep, but I couldn't. I watched my sister as she slept in the twin bed across from me. Her chest rose and fell as she breathed. She was surrounded by a circle of dolls and stuffed animals. One day I teased her about always having to be with so many little friends. Annie told me that they were her best friends because "they're nice and they do whatever I ask them to do."

The more I looked at the stuffed animals and dolls, the more I thought about how Shelly and Nellie always did whatever Dawn told them. I drifted off to sleep for a few minutes and then woke up when I heard my mom in the kitchen. Before I left the room, I hit the floor and tried the splits again. My right knee kept bending and ruining everything. I tried putting my right leg forward. When my left knee collapsed, I wanted to scream. After a few minutes I decided that I had put myself through enough torture and that I'd stretch again later that night.

Walking into the kitchen, I greeted my mother as she sat in a wooden chair at the table with her hat and coat still on. She wrapped her gloves around a mug of coffee and took a sip. "How was practice?" I asked.

My mother tried to smile, but I could tell from her tired eyes that it had been a long morning. "I think we'll do just fine," she said. Then she stood up and limped to the refrigerator.

"What's wrong?" I asked.

"My ankle hurts a little," she said. Then she grabbed her lower back. "And I fell trying to keep up with Jess."

"Are you all right?"

At first I was afraid that my mother had seriously injured herself.

"I'm fine," she insisted.

Okay, not what in the world she was thinking by trying to keep up with my friends?

"So you actually played?" I asked.

"We didn't have enough players."

How embarrassing. Maybe it was better that I wasn't there.

"Your friends said I was a natural on the ice," she added.

I rolled my eyes and she grinned. I watched her as she pulled a box of cereal out of the cupboard and set it on the table. She needed sleep. "Are you sure you can do this, Mom?" I asked.

"Do what?"

"Coach."

"Sure," she said. "It will be fun to learn something new. It will be a challenge, don't you think?"

I nodded.

"Just like it will be a challenge for you to find a way to get along with Dawn," she said.

I had no desire to discuss yesterday's crisis.

"Mr. G. always says today is a new day," I said. "Didn't he tell you that, too?"

She smiled and poured me a bowl of cereal. "You want to go to the school party tonight, don't you?"

"Yes," I said.

"Any problems with Dawn today," she warned, "and you'll be partying by yourself right here."

While I was getting ready for school that morning, I looked into the mirror and started to practice all the lines that I would use on Dawn Miller.

"Do you mind if we switch shoes for a day? Mr. G. said I need to walk in yours for a while. Let's be friends, Dawn. What do you say, pal?"

I cringed. None of my friends would take me seriously. Acting so strangely could really set Dawn off, and then there would be no chance of ever being civil to each other. Not in school. And of course, not at the party that night.

69

Chapter Six

Dawn Miller didn't show up for school the next day, which made for a peaceful day in junior high. It was as if everyone was resting up for the big party that night.

When I arrived home from school, I realized my mother had other plans for me that didn't involve resting, and it had nothing to do with hockey. I would have pretended that I didn't see the list of things to do if it hadn't been taped to the handle of the refrigerator we all raided the second we walked in the door.

I started in the garage, sorting through all the old sneakers, flip-flops, and shoes that lay scattered around the door. I lined them all up in a neat row by size, which turned our garage into a shoe store. Penny always joked that my mom wore boats on her feet, and I looked down at her white nursing shoes and agreed. I lined my dad's shiny size thirteen work shoes next to hers. Then I started the row of muddy and torn sneakers, which easily out-numbered all the other shoes by at least three to one. Frankie's laces were tied, but loose enough for him to slip them on in the case of a quick exit. My tight, triple-knotted laces choked a pair of running shoes that my mother had handed down to me. I picked them up, took in a breath of the stench, winced, and quickly set them in their place. Our best sneakers were either on our feet or hidden in our closets and bedrooms. Leaving my favorite pair of sneakers in public would only be an open invitation for Frankie to accidentally slip them on.

Once I had finished my display, I picked up the mat and shook it. Dust, dirt, and other unknown particles flew up in the air. I held my breath until it all settled, then I pushed the broom over the floor. The door creaked open and my mother set down a sticky bag of garbage.

"Please take this out," she said.

Before I could protest, the door slammed shut. I put on my dad's old gloves and hauled the bag of garbage out to the back and then sprinted through the cold air. I returned to the garage, admired my work, and wished the garage would stay tidy forever. Then I went into the house and pulled out a piece of paper and marker.

PLEASE PICK UP YOUR SHOES!

"What are you doing?" my mom asked.

"If everybody just chipped in a little, I wouldn't have to do all this," I said.

"Your life is so hard, Molly."

Her sarcasm made me want to scream, but I had a party to attend. I taped my sign on the door, returned to the kitchen, washed my hands, and grabbed a piece of pizza. While I was eating, my mom walked out of the bathroom with her hair brushed back and tied into a ponytail. I could tell by her tired eyes and pale face that she did not want to return to work. Before she left, she grabbed a tall round laundry basket and entered each room. With each stop she filled the basket with dirty clothes. When my mother stepped into my room, I held my breath knowing the sight before her eyes. "Molly!" she shouted. "Get in here and clean this up!"

Earlier in the day I had thrown clothes everywhere in my hunt to find something to wear to the party. "I'm going to pick it up!" I yelled. "Would you give me a minute!"

"Now!" she snapped.

I tossed the rest of my pizza in the trash and wiped my face on a towel. As I stormed down the hallway, all I could think of was how much time I spent cleaning the garage and taking out the trash. "I'm a kid," I mumbled. "Not a maid."

My mother's eyes locked onto mine. "Neither am I!"

All right, so maybe it wasn't the smartest thing in the world to say to your mother, especially after she worked ten hours straight and was going back to finish her friend's shift. She went on and on about how we never cleaned up after ourselves and how she was just plain sick and tired of it. "I want this room spotless or no party!" she told me.

I looked at my watch and noted that I had less than

ten minutes to pass her inspection and get dressed or else I'd miss my ride. My father had taken Annie and Ryan to basketball practice, and Kevin was out with friends. If I didn't meet my deadline, my mother would take me back to work with her and make me read a book in the lobby until my father could pick me up. I folded, piled, and tucked things away as quickly as possible. I threw the blanket over my bed and lined up all my stuffed animals and pillows. I ran into the bathroom, brushed my hair and teeth, and put on my favorite sweatshirt and jeans. As I went to my closet and pulled out my hidden sneakers, I called my mother into the room. "Is this good enough?" I asked.

"Fine."

"Thanks, Ma," I said as I ran down the hallway. The horn blared outside.

"Be safe tonight," my mom called out. "I don't want any trouble."

"Okay, yep, gotta go, bye!" I said.

"Molly!" my mother said firmly.

My hand froze on the door handle, and I slowly turned around.

"I mean it," my mother warned. "No trouble at this party."

"Don't worry, Ma," I said. "The parties are boring most of the time."

"All right, I'm trusting you on this one," she said. "Can I at least get a kiss good-bye?"

I shook my head as I walked across the room and gave my mother a quick kiss on the cheek. She smiled and said thanks. I jogged across the room, hoping my friends couldn't see me through the front window. I wondered if their mothers reprimanded them and then insisted on receiving a kiss good-bye. I put my arms in my coat as I stomped down the small sidewalk and headed toward the car. I pulled open the door and sat down. I looked up, ready to protest about wacky mothers, but stopped as I stared at Wil sitting right next to me. She pushed her blue-rimmed glasses back and asked, "What's bugging you?"

My mind filled with guilt as I looked at a friend who did not have a mother to complain about anymore. I stared at the seat in front of me and mumbled, "Nothing."

"You know, Dawn's going to be at the party," Wil said. "Are you going to be all right?"

I rolled my eyes and groaned. "I talked to Mr. Gordon about this already," I said. "Things are just fine. Why doesn't everyone leave us alone?"

"Sorry," Wil said. "I didn't know you and Dawn had made up."

I glared at my friend to let her know I was not in the mood. "Drop it, Wil."

All this talk of people anticipating bad behavior and problems made me more determined to prove them wrong. Rico dropped us off and we jogged up the steps to the main doors of the Tucker Park District building.

"The DJ had better be good," Penny said, "or we're outta here."

"If it gets boring," I said, "we can always go to the church and play ball after my brother's practice."

"Sounds good to me," Rosie said.

I looked at Rosie, who was dressed in her best jeans, a

Yankees sweatshirt, and one of Rico's baseball caps. The last thing Rosie wanted to do at a school party was be forced to dance with the rest of us.

"You got your dancing shoes on tonight, Ro?" Penny joked, but Rosie did not reply.

As we waited in line for our hands to be stamped, Anita joined us. I watched her as she slouched and started biting her nails. A lot of kids teased Anita for being so tall. She never asked for any extra attention, but everyone gave it to her. I followed her stare out to the dance floor, which was mostly filled with girls. I remembered how nervous I had been when I was in sixth grade and used to come to the school dances. I had a big-time secret crush on a boy in the eighth grade named Andy Maggiano. My friends would beg me to dance, but I never would when he was around. I wondered if boys ever did dumb things like that around girls they thought were cute.

"Hey, hey!" J. J. announced as he burst through the doors. "The man of the hour has arrived."

"Oh, yeah?" Penny called out. "Where is he?"

Everyone started to laugh. Eddie and some other eighth-grade boys came in a few minutes later. Right behind them were Dawn, Shelly, and Nellie all dressed in rainbow-colored shirts, tight black pants, and black high heels with rainbow-colored bows in their hair. From across the room I could see their blue eye shadow and bright red lipstick. They held open the door for the kids behind them. I looked carefully to see whom they were being so nice to. When Jessica Wilson walked in with a big smile on her face, and a rainbow-colored bow in her hair, I almost passed out. "Did Jess come with Dawn?" I asked Anita in a weak whisper.

"I don't know," Anita said as she looked at the crowd. "But it sure looks like it."

"Let's go get the party started," Penny said, and she pulled me toward the auditorium.

The music started thumping. Penny and Wil started rocking as we moved across the dance floor. Penny walked up to the disc jockey and put in her favorite requests, but I couldn't think about anything else other than seeing Jessica, our team captain, with Dawn. "Did you see that?" I asked Wil.

"What?" Wil smiled as she bent her knees, rocked, and bumped Rosie on the hip. Rosie almost tipped over. "Come on, Rosie," Wil said. "Get loose!"

I started to move with the music a little bit and then snap my fingers. Penny ran back into our group, and I wanted to tell her about the alarming situation, but she had already started dancing. The DJ dimmed the lights and we all started to loosen up. Even Anita stopped biting her fingernails and started grooving to the beat. Slowly I began to forget about Dawn.

"Go 'Nita, go 'Nita," we all cheered.

Then Dawn, Shelly, Nellie, and Jess barged into our circle. My muscles tightened as they laughed and joked around as if we were all friends. I looked at Wil and she raised her eyebrows and shrugged. Penny kept smiling as if nothing was wrong. I took a deep breath and hoped for no trouble. Then Dawn started cheering, "Go, big girl, go, big girl!" The others joined in. I cringed, knowing how much Anita hated being called "big girl."

"Bend your knees so we can see you!" Dawn yelled.

Anita's arms stopped moving, and she stared at the ground. Her smile faded and she slouched as she walked out of the middle of the circle. I turned to Jessica, who had a big smile on her face.

"She's our teammate!" I yelled. "Don't laugh at her!"

Jess didn't even hear me. She kept dancing along with everyone else. I went right up to the real bad apple and screamed over the music, "Nobody invited you into our circle!"

Dawn held the palm of her hand in front of my face and stuck her nose in the air.

"You're such a—" I began.

"Let's go, Molly," Rosie interrupted, pulling me away. "I've got to go use the rest room."

Rosie threw all her body weight into pulling me away. I stared at Dawn as I walked out of the gym. She stared back, winked, and grinned. Then she walked over to the boys and started dancing with them. Rosie kept pulling on me and I yelled, "Let go!"

Rosie was pretty strong for being about half my weight. After she pushed me into the bathroom, she turned around and said, "I didn't want you to get into trouble."

I scoffed and said, "Thanks, Ro. But I'm a big girl—big enough to fight my own battles."

"When you get mad, she wins," Rosie reminded me.

"Who are you?" I shot back. "Angel? Mr. G.? My mom?"

Within seconds Penny, Wil, and Anita were all in the bathroom.

"What's up?" they asked.

My friends washed their hands and fixed their hair as if they enjoyed being in a smelly public rest room. Nobody talked about Dawn, who was the person responsible for sending us there. None of them even mentioned how our team captain was hanging out with our biggest rival.

"This is stupid," I said. "I'm going home."

"How are you going to get there?" Penny asked.

"I'll walk. It's not that cold out."

"But it's dark," Rosie said.

"I'll walk over to the church and play basketball with my dad and his friends," I said. "They stay late and play after they're finished coaching."

I left the bathroom and went out to the auditorium to find my coat. J. J. came up to me and asked, "Are you leaving already?"

I nodded.

"Where are you going?" he asked.

"To the church to play ball," I said.

"Can I come?"

I picked up my coat, turned and left the building, too angry at Dawn to answer. I could still hear the music as I jogged down the dark street all alone. The sweat running down my back felt cool. I couldn't wait to see my dad and be in the gym. I'd stay up all night and he'd rebound for me as I shot all my troubles away.

"Wait up!" a voice called out. Heavy breathing and the pounding of several feet followed me.

"You didn't have to come," I said as I looked at my friends. "Go back. You were having fun."

"I wasn't," Anita said.

"Me neither," Rosie added.

I looked at Wil and Penny. If they said they weren't having fun, it would be a lie.

"We'd rather be playing ball," Penny said.

"I'm so sick of those parties anyway," Wil added.

"Did you see Jess and Dawn hanging out together?" I asked.

"Are you sure?" Wil sounded as surprised as I was.

"They walked in together," I said. "They all had the same cute little outfits and stupid bows!"

"Jess is too smart to be hanging out with Dawn," Penny said. "I'm sure she was just trying to be nice."

"She'd better not quit our team to play on Dawn's," I said.

"I think Penny's right, Molly," Rosie agreed. "Don't sweat it."

I breathed a sigh of relief and then continued on down the city streets with my friends by my side. I looked in the distance and saw the gym lights on in St. Michael's church. We cut through the alley and went in the back door. I carefully peeked through the tiny windows to make sure my brother's practice had ended. My dad had taught us how to enter a gym with respect: "Slowly open the door to see what's going on, make sure you're not interrupting, walk in quietly, and ask permission." My dad was an over-thirty-year-old league gym rat and an expert at negotiating gym time.

"Hi, Dad," I said as we walked in. "Do you mind if we play at the other end?"

He shook his head. "Come on in. How was the party?"

"Boring with a capital *B*," Wil said. "We're getting too old for that kid stuff anyway."

I politely asked my brother Frankie if I could use his basketball. To my amazement, he passed it to me.

"Thanks," I mumbled.

We took off our coats and threw them on the stage, then played ball in our jeans and sweaters. Penny put Annie on her team and Frankie on mine. For about twenty minutes we played without an argument even though I almost lost it when Penny's team scored the last point and won 11–9. After the game I shook everybody's hands but didn't say "good game." I just headed toward the water fountain to cool off.

In between games I watched my dad play down at the other end with his buddies from work. He jumped and grunted as he snagged rebounds and made hard passes to his teammates. When he missed a few easy shots, he started yelling at himself, "Come on! You're terrible!" I wanted to yell out, "That's okay, Dad! Good try! Hang in there!" I felt so bad for him, seeing how hard he was on himself. It didn't look like he was having any fun.

"Hey, hey!" a voice called out. I turned to the doors and saw J. J. strut in with his oversize black coat and baggy black jeans.

"Did you bring the man of the hour this time?" Penny asked with a grin.

Eddie followed J. J. into the gym. "Try man of the year," Eddie said. "I know you've all been waiting for me."

"Ugh," I moaned.

"How come you left the party?" Wil asked the boys.

"You didn't hear what happened with Dawn?" Eddie said.

"Hear what?" I asked.

"We'll only tell you if we can play," J. J. said with a grin.

"Oh, come on, J.," I said.

"Well?" he asked.

"You're in," Penny decided, eager to hear the details.

All of us gathered around and waited for the news. J. J. slowly took off his coat and neatly hung it on the back of a chair.

"Do you mind if we go get a drink of water first?" he asked. "It's a long story."

"No water until you talk," Wil said.

He huffed. "Dawn started dancing with Jason Watson."

"Shelly's boyfriend?" Wil gasped.

J. J. nodded. "Shelly got mad at Dawn, so she went into the bathroom and started writing *DMs* all over the place. The monitors went into the bathroom and saw Dawn's initials, so they threw her out."

"You're lying," Wil said.

"Nope. Dawn started screaming at Shelly and Nellie like she had lost her mind. The next thing you know, Dawn tells Jason to leave with her, and he follows her like a dog right out the door."

"For real?" Penny asked.

"Yep," J. J. said. "Dawn started telling off the monitors, so they called security. But by the time they got there, she was already gone."

"What did Shelly and Nellie do?" I asked.

"They told everybody all the things Dawn's been

doing to them like stealing their gym clothes, taking their homework—everything."

"So she doesn't have any friends now!" I said excitedly.

"Except for one," Eddie said as he dribbled over to us.

"Who?" Rosie asked.

"Jessica Wilson," he said. "Jess left the party with Dawn, too."

I couldn't believe my ears. "You're lying!"

"I'm not kidding," he said. "Tell 'em, J."

"It's true," J. J. assured us.

I turned to my friends, who all stood with their mouths open and eyes wide. "What are we going to do?" I asked.

A few seconds of shock passed.

"Let's just wait and see," Penny suggested. "This could all blow over."

"Shelly and Nellie will probably be carrying Dawn's books around on Monday," Wil said. "Don't think this will change anything."

"What about Jess?" I said.

"She's still on our team," Wil said, "unless she tells us otherwise. And Jess doesn't seem like she's a traitor."

As we started the second game, I played in a daze for the first few minutes. But when Eddie blocked my shot, I woke up fast. Of course, with Penny on my team, we won. At the end of the game, my dad walked over and said, "Are you girls excited about your first hockey game on Sunday?"

Everyone stopped running and dribbling. All eyes turned toward my dad.

"What'd you say, Mr. O.?" Wil asked nervously.

"Your game on Sunday morning against the Foothill Flames," he said.

"Nobody told us about a game this weekend," I said.

"Yeah," my dad said. "You start on Sunday at seven A.M."

My mind raced with the memories of my belly flop and the overall disaster that we called our first scrimmage. None of us had the proper equipment. We didn't even have uniforms.

"Are they any good?" I asked.

My dad nodded. "Everybody in the league is good."

"Except us," Wil said.

We had about thirty-two hours to gather equipment, find some uniforms, make some plays, and try to look like a team. Those tasks were small in comparison to answering the biggest question that ran through all of our minds: Was Jessica Wilson still with us?

Chapter Seven

The first thing I did when I woke up the next morning was go to the phone book and look up Jessica Wilson's number. I picked up the phone and dialed quickly. A woman answered with a loud "Hello!" She sounded like my mom always did after one of us tracked mud across a clean kitchen floor. It had to be Mrs. Wilson.

"May I speak to Jessica?" I asked nervously.

"She's not allowed to use the phone," she replied.

On any other day I would have said thank you and goodbye. But this was different. Mrs. Wilson had to bend the rules just this once. Our team's future depended on it. "This is an emergency," I insisted.

"Oh, really," Mrs. Wilson said curiously. "Who is this?"

"Molly O'Malley," I replied. "Jess is on our hockey

team. I wanted to let her know that we have a game tomorrow."

"She won't be going," her mother said firmly.

I almost dropped the phone. "Excuse me?" I asked in disbelief.

"She broke curfew last night," her mother explained.

A second of silence passed as I pieced the puzzle together. The story about Dawn's getting into trouble and Jess's leaving the party with her had to be true. Mrs. Wilson must have been mad at Dawn for getting her daughter in trouble, but she didn't understand. *The girls on the hockey team are the good girls. We had nothing to do with it. Jess should be hanging out with girls like us!*

"I'm sorry," I said. "We left the party early. I didn't know Jess got into trouble."

"Well, she did," her mother said impatiently.

"Are you sure she can't play tomorrow?"

"Yes, I'm sure," Mrs. Wilson snapped.

"We really need her," I pleaded. "She's our captain."

"Until she starts acting like a leader, you won't be seeing much of her," her mother said firmly. *Click.* I froze in shock. I held the receiver in my hand and then slowly set the phone back on the hook.

"Ahhhh!" I screamed in frustration.

My mom walked into the kitchen. "What's wrong?"

"Jess is grounded!" I exclaimed. "She can't come to the game tomorrow!"

"That's all right," my mother said.

"No, it's not!" I said. "Parents can be so difficult sometimes. No offense, but what's one hockey game? It's not like we're the ones who got her in trouble. Dawn did!"

"We've got other things to worry about," my mother said.

"Like what?" I asked.

"We don't have enough equipment for everyone to play tomorrow," she said.

"We've got helmets, skates, and sticks." I said.

"What about pads and gloves?" she asked.

I walked over to the phone and started calling the Ballplayers to meet at my house for an emergency meeting. No matter what my mother said, the details on the equipment could be put on the back burner. When the Ballplayers arrived, I broke the news to them about having to play without Jess.

"She's still on our team, isn't she?" Wil asked.

"Yeah," I said. "I think she's only grounded for the weekend."

"That's not what Eddie said," J. J. disagreed.

"What'd he say?" I asked.

"Dawn's trying to get Jess to play with the Sharks still."

"Do you believe that liar?" I hoped it wasn't true.

J. J. nodded. "He wasn't kidding around this time."

I rolled my eyes and threw my hands up in the air. "What are we going to do?"

"Who cares?" Penny said. "I'm tired of talking about this so much. Let's just play!"

"There's only one other slight problem," I said. "We still don't have enough equipment."

"What do we need?" Wil asked.

I showed her the list. "We need ten of everything. Just

get as much as possible of anything and everything you can find. Be creative."

EQUIPMENT WE NEED:
Shin guards
Long socks or sweatpants
Pants
Thigh pads in pants
Shoulder pads
Elbow pads
Jerseys
Helmets
Gloves
Goalie equipment

"Looks like a good ol' treasure hunt to me!" Penny said.

"Losers have to wash the winners' uniforms all season," J. J. added.

We split up into teams and set out in the neighborhood and streets to come up with what we needed. Two hours later we piled all our belongings on the table. Wil had the list and a pencil in her hand.

"Well," she began. "Let's see. Team number one came up with some interesting equipment. Basketball knee pads as elbow pads, smelly football jerseys for our uniforms, and a baseball mitt for a goalie glove. Team number two dug up a bunch of filthy soccer shin guards and a bunch of tape."

"What's with this stack of magazines?" Wil asked.

"It looks like we don't have enough football pants with pads," Penny said. "So some of us are going to have to tape the magazines to our thighs," Penny said.

"That will look cool," Wil muttered as she scanned down the list. Some of the treasures included big gloves from the fire department, a catcher's mask, football shoulder pads, pillows, and Ace bandages. "So it looks like we have most of what we need," Wil said.

"If we need anything else, I'll go to the used sporting goods store," I said.

"We've already been there," Rosie said.

"What did you buy?" I asked.

"Nothing," she said. "We went through the garbage out back. That's where we got most of this stuff."

We all groaned.

"At least we have everything," I said.

"Which team won the treasure hunt?" Rosie asked.

"It looks like the score was about even," Wil said.

"Let's just worry about winning tomorrow," Penny added.

On our way to the rink on Sunday morning, conversation was kept to a minimum. It had nothing to do with our being nervous. We were experiencing some difficulty in adjusting to the early morning routine.

"Did everybody eat breakfast?" my mother asked as we walked into the building.

"No," Wil said. "I had to get in an extra five minutes of sleep."

My mother handed out bagels and we headed toward the locker room. J. J. stopped in front of the Women sign and said, "Does this mean me, too?" He grinned at the rest of us. None of us laughed.

"In here with me," Rico said as he leaned against the men's room door.

We hauled our laundry and army bags into the dingy locker room and started unpacking. I looked at the pile of pads and equipment and didn't know where to start.

"Can somebody help me put my pants on?" Rosie asked. "Where do all these pads go?"

Wil took charge and started calling out the order of dressing. "Shin guards, socks or sweatpants, or tape, padded pants if you have them, magazines if you don't, skates, shoulder pads, elbow pads or knee pads, jersey, helmet, and gloves last. Let's race."

"Ready, set, go!" I called out.

Equipment flew all over the locker room. We screamed at each other for help and then complained when our teammates wouldn't move fast enough. Penny snapped her helmet on and grimaced as she pulled her gloves over her hands.

"I'm done!" she said.

Right after Wil tightened her last knot, she said, "Uh-oh!"

"What's wrong?" I asked.

"I have to use the rest room," she said.

We all shook our heads as Wil removed her equipment one piece at a time. I looked at Angel and noticed she was fussing with her skates.

"You all right?" I asked.

"Yeah," she said. "They're just too tight."

Penny sat down next to her and tried to help. "If your feet start to hurt, you don't have to play."

I turned to Anita, who stood biting her nails.

"Let me help you put your gloves on before you chew off your fingers," I said.

We emerged from the locker room like a bunch of hobbling old ladies. J. J. waited for us as we leaned against the wall and held on to the railing. I looked up at the ice and saw the Foothill Flames putting on a show. Dressed in their bright yellow uniforms with red flames, they zoomed through warm-ups and weaved through fancy drills. I pushed open the wooden door and stepped up on the ice. The Flames coach was asking me, "Where are the Broadway Ballplayers?"

"We're the Ballplayers," I said.

His mouth dropped open as he checked out our mismatched jerseys, football pants, fire gloves, and layers of tape. "Oh," he said. "Sorry."

I scowled at the man as he turned and skated away.

"Let's warm up," I said. We hustled out on to the ice and passed the puck around. Wil fell twice, I hit the deck once, and Angel ran into the wall. After each spill, people in the stands started to laugh.

"Did you girls get your uniforms at the dump?" a man yelled.

I glared at the man and turned back to the action.

"Come on!" I yelled at my teammates. "Let's win!"

I yelled so hard that I lost my balance and fell. Anita came over and helped pick me up. When I stood up, I saw the Flames huddle in one group at their end, so I called everyone together. We zigged and zagged our way into the middle, trying not to run into each other.

"Let's bring it in!" I said. "Win on three. One, two, three . . . win!"

We skated over to our coaches. Rico called out the lines, which he explained were mass substitutions.

"Everybody'll be shifting in and out on the fly," he began. "So pay attention, be ready to go in, and play as hard as you can when you're out there."

Then my mom finished the pep talk by yelling, "Let's go, Broadway! Let's show 'em!"

My nerves tingled as our small crowd of five family members and fans cheered. Then I heard a huge roar at the other end. The Flames had taken the ice, and the stands full of fans started chanting and clapping to the chant, "Fire and ice! Fire and ice!"

"That's catchy," Wil said. "We need a little something like that."

The Flames caught on fire real fast. Two minutes into the game I blinked and the puck was in the goal. I fell to the ground and punched the ice with my glove.

"You'll get the next one, Molly!" Penny called out.

I kept my body glued to the ground.

"Yeah!" Wil said as she stood over me. "Now get up, because everyone is staring at you."

I pulled myself up and hoped my mask hid the tears in my eyes. Thirty seconds later the fire continued. Slap shot, rebound, wrist shot, rebound, pass, score. I started throwing my body around, grunting and groaning. I screamed at Anita and Wil for some help. All Wil kept saying was "I'm trying! I'm trying!" All Anita said was "I'm sorry! I'm really sorry!"

Penny and J. J. came to the rescue a few times and held on to the puck just long enough for me to catch my breath. By the end of the first period, the score was 3-0.

Rico and my mom tried to diagram a new strategy on the board in the locker room at the break.

"Just please keep them away from me!" I pleaded.

My toes were frozen solid in my skates. Back in the goal, I danced around, drifting back and forth just to keep myself warm. When Penny scored on the opening power play, I kept skating around in front of the goal hoping that it was bringing us luck. But that was our only highlight. The Flames came at me like a bunch of hot missiles and scored three goals in the third period. I thrashed myself around and screamed at the refs for letting players on the other team crash into Penny and Rosie.

"Why don't you call it both ways?" I yelled.

"Watch it, goalie," the ref warned. "Or you're going to spend some quality time in the box."

I gave up on the pathetic refs and focused on my job. Half the time I couldn't even see the puck with all the people crowding me. I yelled for help. I called out for answers. Nobody came to the rescue. We were humiliated 6–1.

"That was an easy practice," one Flame said.

I glared at her. "Our best player wasn't here," I shot back.

"You think that she would have made a difference?" another Flame asked.

I skated away mad at Jess for not being there, angry at Dawn for getting her into trouble, and disgusted by my rotten performance.

"Look at it this way," my mom said in the locker room. "We scored the same number of points as them in the third period."

"If we played them all game like we did in the last few minutes," Rico added, "we could have won."

We all sat in the locker room unable to look at one another. I wanted to stand up and apologize to everyone for being so bad in goal. I shouldn't have yelled so much at everyone. I wanted to tell them I was sorry. It was all my fault.

"See you at practice tomorrow," Rico said.

Penny, Wil, and J. J. started joking around a little later, but I didn't talk to anyone. I just wanted to get into the car and go home.

"Come on, Molly," my mom said. "We're going to church."

"Do we have to?" I asked.

"Yes," she said and she handed me some clothes to change into. "Your father is waiting for us in the car."

I handed my mother my bag of equipment and returned to the locker room all by myself. I slammed into the door in protest, and then stopped when I saw Angel on the bench massaging her feet. She stood up quickly and tried to put on her shoe.

"You don't have to play if your feet hurt," I said.

She pulled the hood over her thick black hair. I knew how much Angel's feet hurt after running cross-country and playing soccer. I wasn't sure if her doctor or her parents knew about her playing hockey. Whenever we brought up the conversation about how her mom and dad felt about anything, she always changed the subject.

"We won't have enough players if I don't," she said.

"I'll get some others," I said. "I don't want you to hurt yourself anymore."

I could see the tears well in her green eyes as she limped past me. I changed into my clothes and tried to think of anybody who was willing to play with a team that just got beat 6–1.

The thoughts of our team problems stayed with me as I sat through church. As the choir sang and the organ droned, I kept telling myself that I shouldn't be thinking of all my sports worries during church. I tried following along with the songs and repeating the words the priest said in his readings. I looked up at my mom and dad and watched as they paid attention and listened. What were they thinking about? I closed my eyes and asked for forgiveness for many things. Maybe I did overreact about Jess not being at our game. I started to think about Dawn and felt mad and frustrated. I looked around at all the signs of peacefulness and knew that I shouldn't be having those feelings. I pictured Mr. Gordon reprimanding me in his office, my father throwing the towel into the sink, and my mom yelling at me for my messy room. I wanted to say that these things wouldn't happen ever again. I knew that I was wrong, but I couldn't bring myself to stop thinking about how much Dawn, Eddie, and losing made me miserable. So I opened up to the pages of the song we were singing and belted out a few verses. But it didn't make me feel any better.

Jessica didn't show at practice on Monday morning.

"You'd think she would have at least called," Wil said.

"My dad doesn't let me speak to anyone when I'm grounded," Rosie said. "Maybe she's still in trouble."

I wondered how long the trouble would last. I couldn't

handle another loss. We stepped on the ice and went through a bunch of the same, simple drills. I fell three times in less than five minutes. The last fall resembled the belly flop I had performed in front of Dawn and Eddie the week before.

"Would you stop beating yourself up!" Wil said.

"You're dangerous," Angel added.

At the end of practice, the whistle blew and the Zamboni machine came out to clear the ice. As it moved slowly over the ice, the loud machine left a smooth, glassy surface behind.

"We should call you the Zamboni," J. J. said to me. "You spend more time cleaning the ice than you do standing up straight."

I started off the school day by dropping a whole stack of books and papers in front of my locker. I rushed to pick up my mess while I frantically scanned the hallway for Jess. She wasn't around. As I pushed open the bathroom door, I heard two girls yelling at each other. I turned the corner and stopped right in front of Shelly and Nellie. To my surprise they were without Dawn. They stopped their conversation and stared at me. Neither of them said another word while I was in the girls' room. After I left, I turned the corner and ran right into the queen bully herself.

"I heard you lost a close one yesterday," she said.

"I heard you have no friends," I shot back.

She scowled at me. "Then how come Jess wants to play on my team and not yours?"

Frustration rippled through me. I was so angry I couldn't speak.

"She doesn't want to hurt your feelings by telling you the truth," Dawn continued.

"I'll go ask her myself!" I said. "Where is she?"

"She's sick today," Dawn said. "She called me last night."

My ears went numb. No way was Jess a traitor.

"Get to class!" a lunch monitor said. "Now!"

I turned away from Dawn and walked down the hall-way. On my way to class, I passed Eddie. He swiped Billy's comb out of his back pocket.

"Give it back, Eddie!" I yelled.

Eddie laughed as Billy chased him around. I ran over to him and grabbed on to his arm. I gritted my teeth as I pulled on his tight fist. "You could really be a good guy, Eddie," I said. "I've seen you with your little sister. I've seen how nice you can be. Why do you have to be so rotten?"

He looked at me in shock. For once he didn't say something mean. Within seconds Eddie released his grip and handed Billy's comb back to him. The bell rang and we all sprinted into our classrooms.

I went to math class and wrote Penny a quick note. It read:

Dear P.,
Do you know what's up with Shelly and Nellie? Have you heard if they're still mad at Dawn? I just saw her and she says Jess is afraid to tell me that she doesn't want to play with us. I'm calling Jess when I get home today.

Molly

I didn't care how sick Jess was. I needed an answer.

Chapter Eight

Would you hurry up?" I asked Frankie as he held the receiver in his hand. He had no reason to be on the phone unless he was talking to our grandparents. "Who are you talking to?" I asked.

He glared at me and said, "None of your business!" Then he sat down on our sofa and smiled as he continued his meaningless conversation with some unidentified friend.

"Please," I begged quietly, knowing he was staying on the phone just to get under my skin. "I'm sorry. I just really have to use the phone. It's an emergency!"

He wouldn't hang up. As he talked and smiled, I didn't say anything. I just waited for him to relax before I made my move. Frankie tilted his head back in laughter and closed his eyes for a brief second. I hopped up from my seat, reached across the end table and *click!* Frankie stopped midsentence and screamed, "I'm telling!"

"Time is up!" I said firmly as he grabbed my arm and tugged on my shoulder. "I asked you nicely, but you didn't listen!"

After a few seconds Kevin came in the room and broke us up. He told Frankie that he could use the TV remote if he let me use the phone. It was a done deal. I picked up the phone and made the big call to Jessica Wilson.

Her mother answered again. I asked for Jess and she said, "She's sick. May I take a message?"

I bought some time with a "Umm, yeah, I guess" while I went back and forth over whether I should press Mrs. Wilson on the details. *How bad is she? Will she be back to practice on Wednesday? Has she been to a doctor? Is she still on our team?*

"This is Molly O'Malley," I began. "I was just wondering if Jess was still on our hockey team or not."

Mrs. Wilson paused for a moment and then slowly said, "I think so." My heart skipped a beat. She didn't sound convincing.

"Is she going to be at practice on Wednesday?" I asked.

"If she feels better, she will." she said.

"She should be fine, by Wednesday," I asked. "Right?"

"I don't know yet," she replied.

I lost all patience. Jess could play. She had to be hiding something from us. "If she doesn't want to be on our team anymore, she can just tell me. Can you ask her that?"

"Right now?" Mrs. Wilson asked in disbelief.

I slowly began to back off. "If now is not a good time . . ."

"I'm not waking her up," Mrs. Wilson insisted.

I could tell by her sharp tone that I had pressed a bit too much. "That's okay," I said quickly. "I'm sorry, Mrs. Wilson. I'll just talk to Jess when I see her. Sorry about all the trouble. Thanks."

I hung up the phone and collapsed on the sofa. Annie came up to me and said, "What's the matter, Molly?"

I just shook my head. I was at a loss for words. I couldn't believe how crazy I had become over this whole mess. *Did wanting to win so badly mean that something was wrong with me? Should I go see the doctor? Yes, I should. Wait. I need a second opinion.* I picked up the phone, called Penny, and told her that Mrs. Wilson wouldn't let me talk to Jess.

"You asked her even though you knew she was sick and sleeping?" Penny said.

"Yeah," I said. "She can't be that sick. She had plenty of energy to run around with Dawn on Friday night and then talk to her on Sunday."

"But maybe she is really sick," Penny said softly.

Then I started to feel bad all over again. I don't know what I was thinking. Penny didn't panic like me. She always smiled when she was under pressure. I trembled. My best friend hardly broke a sweat. I couldn't dry off. She wasn't stressing over Jess or Dawn. I could feel my nerves winding up.

As I hung up the phone, I started to accept that something was definitely wrong with me. Then I thought of Dawn Miller and how much she would brag to me every day for the rest of the year if her team won.

"Do we have any chicken soup?" I asked my sister.

"I don't know," my sister replied. "Why?"

"I might take some over to Jessica," I said. "She hasn't been feeling very well."

After missing two consecutive days of school, Wednesday morning would be the moment of truth for our team captain. If she had any sense of commitment and loyalty, she would report to our practice regardless of any illness. I sat on the bench of the ice-cold rink at 5:51 A.M., tied up my skates, and checked the clock every thirty seconds.

"Where is she?" I pleaded to Penny.

"Relax, Molly," Penny said. "Don't sweat it."

Just as I started to warm up, I turned around and spotted Jessica push through the front door and head toward the locker room.

"Sorry I'm late!" she yelled. "I'll be out in a minute!"

I flashed a relieved smile and then yelled, "Take your time!"

Forget my stress. What's another five minutes? I took my spot in goal and started cheering for my teammates as we warmed up. "Let's go, Broadway! Way to hustle, P.! Nice pass, J.!"

Wil and Anita both stopped, rested their sticks on the ice, and looked at me. "What's gotten into you?" Wil asked.

"We're going to win this weekend," I said. "I just know it! I feel it!"

From that point forward, practice was all downhill. Rico called out fancy plays, and we had no idea what he was talking about. People started asking the same questions over and over, which made half the team click their tongues and roll their eyes. "Come on," I said in frustration. "Maybe if we all listened!"

"Yeah," Jess added. "It's not that hard!"

"Maybe for you it's not!" Wil muttered. "But I'm not trying out for the Olympics this year, all right?"

The coaches started yelling at us to "Pay attention!" We weaved through drills, and the team took turns at shots on goal. Even without a goalie, only two of us hit the puck into the net. Wil wiped out on one play, which sent contagious giggles around to some of our team-mates. While Anita, Wil, and Penny were laughing, Jess, J. J., and I were going all out on each play. "Can we be serious for more than five minutes!" I screamed.

The more they laughed, the harder I pushed myself. But even during the plays when we all hustled and paid attention, we still looked like clowns in a circus. Jess started to shake her head at all of us. Trying to make up for our lack of skill, I cheered extra loud when Penny scored on a fast break and after J. J.'s sweet assist. But nothing made Jess smile. With every mistake we made, she gave up more and more. By the end of practice she was just drifting around the ice with a scowl on her face.

"Hustle!" I screamed. "That means everybody!"

The whistle blew and we huddled into the middle of the ice. I stared at Jess the entire time. She wouldn't look at me or anyone else. When we all piled our gloves together for a team cheer, Jess didn't say a word. She skated off the ice and went directly to the locker room.

"What's wrong with her?" I asked.

"She's probably still sick," Penny said.

"Sick of us," Wil quipped.

BEEP! BEEP! BEEP! The engine of the Zamboni revved, and we cleared the ice. "There's your favorite machine," Wil joked. I didn't laugh. Our captain's foot was halfway out the door.

My dad walked into the kitchen dressed in his blue police uniform. Annie followed right behind him wearing his police hat over her messy hair.

"Good morning," my dad said. My mom had left for work right after practice, and it was up to all of us to get ready for school. When Annie crawled onto my dad's lap as he sat down at the table, he told her politely to get dressed. Then Frankie finished his breakfast and went into his room. Kevin brushed his teeth, grabbed his bag and flew out the back door. I took my time eating and enjoyed the few minutes I would have to spend with my dad before school.

"How's hockey?" he asked.

"We had a bad practice this morning," I said. "Everyone is mad at each other because we lost, and no one seems to know what to do. Jess is a lot better than we are."

"Hang in there," he said. "Most of the kids you're playing against have been on the ice since they were little. You can't expect to learn it all in less than a month."

"I know," I muttered.

"How are things going with Dawn?" he asked.

I hesitated knowing that he would be paying close attention to my response.

"She got in trouble on Friday night at the party," I said. "But we weren't there. And believe it or not, I had nothing to do with it."

He smiled.

"Now Shelly and Nellie are really mad," I added. "Dawn doesn't seem to have very many friends except . . ."

I couldn't leak to my dad about how Dawn was actively recruiting Jess to quit our team and play with the Sharks. He would automatically link me as a potential suspect for trouble.

My dad looked up as he sipped his cup of coffee and waited. I stared at his two crooked broken fingers. Then he set his cup down and asked, "Except who?"

". . . a few kids," I finished.

He stood up and limped over to the sink. His knees always paid the price for an early rise after a late-night basketball game. "Did your team win last night?" I asked.

"No," he said. "We lost again."

I began to feel like our whole family was being afflicted with some sort of losing disease. Instead of talking about it, we turned to my second least-favorite subject.

"How are you getting along with Eddie?" my father asked.

"I don't know," I replied. "Something really strange happened the other day when he was picking on Billy. I ran up to Eddie and yelled at him about how he didn't have to be so mean."

"What made you say that?"

"I saw him with his little sister that morning and he was actually nice to her. I didn't understand why he couldn't be nice to somebody besides his sister."

My dad smiled and shook his head. I didn't like it when he did that because he would never tell me what he was thinking.

"What did Eddie say when you said that to him?" my dad asked.

"He just kind of looked at me in shock and he stopped picking on Billy," I said. "It was weird. I couldn't believe I said it and neither could Eddie."

"I'm sure Eddie appreciated what you said to him."

My father made it sound like I cared about Eddie after all the rotten things he did. "I still don't like him," I insisted.

My dad sighed and he sat down next to me. "I'm not saying you have to be best friends with him or anybody else," he began, "but you've got to show a little respect."

The last word I would ever use as a way to deal with bullies like Eddie or Dawn was *respect*. "They have no respect for anyone else," I said. "Why should I give it to them? Do you respect the people you throw in jail?"

My dad listened as I blew off some steam.

"I put people in jail because it's my job," he said. "It's not up to me to decide what that person does or does not deserve. That's up to the courts."

"But don't you just get so mad sometimes when criminals get away with so much?" I asked.

He nodded. "I do, but there is only so much I can do. If I go around disrespecting people, then it's only going to make them care about others less."

This all sounded good, but I'd seen shows on television about police officers who lost all their cool. I'd seen my dad's temper and how things became personal when it came to protecting innocent people.

"What am I supposed to do?" I asked.

"Try to show a little respect and you might get some in

return," he explained. "I know it's hard. But look at the results. You did it for Eddie and he responded."

On the way to school I thought of all the different ways I could strike a respectful conversation with Dawn Miller.

"All your writing on the bathroom walls is really good, Dawn," I would say. *"You should think of joining the art club."*

"Why don't you take a break from stealing lunch money today, and I'll give you half of my sandwich. I wasn't really hungry anyway."

I laughed at myself. There was no way in the world I could say any of these things. Such a sudden change in attitude would freak out my friends.

"What are you laughing at?" Penny asked.

"Nothin'," I said.

Just as we walked off the bus, I spotted Shelly and Nellie whispering in the doorway of school. They both wore bright blue shirts, jeans, and matching socks. When they looked our way and waved us over, the Ballplayers and I looked at each other.

"Are they waving at us?" Wil asked as she looked over her shoulder.

"Penny, Molly, all of you come here!" Nellie's voice boomed.

Slowly we walked up the steps and waited for them to talk.

"Do you need any players for your hockey team?" Shelly asked.

I looked at Penny. She turned to them and asked, "Why?"

"Because we want to play," Nellie explained. "And Dawn won't let us try out for the Sharks."

A moment of silence passed. "We'll have to check with our coaches."

We all smiled in shock and walked away from the conversation. A few seconds passed and Wil blurted out, "Am I dreaming or did they just ask to play on our team?"

"They're doing this to get back at Dawn," I said.

"Yeah," Penny said. "I don't like the sound of this."

I quickly gathered my books for class and ducked into the rest room before the bell rang. After I washed my hands, I rushed out the door and almost ran smack into Dawn. I noticed that for once she wasn't dressed in the same colors as Shelly and Nellie. She glared at me with her beady eyes and pushed me up against the wall.

"What do you want?" I asked.

"How come you asked Shelly and Nellie to play on your team?"

"I didn't!" I said.

"Yeah, you did," she snarled.

I sidestepped past her and spun around. Now her back was against the wall. Nothing my father and I had discussed entered my mind. Just as I raised my finger to tell her off, Mr. G. commanded, "Get to class!"

Dawn muttered, "I'll take care of this later," and strutted down the hallway. I froze knowing that my class was in the direction of Mr. Gordon, and he was still staring right at me.

"Good morning, Mr. G.," I said with a nervous smile as I tried to walk on by.

"May I speak with you for a moment?" he asked. I stopped and looked up at him. "What was the problem there?"

"Nothin'," I said. "We were just talking."

He raised his eyebrows and rested his hand on his hip. "I hope you were just talking," he added.

"This is just crazy," I said.

"I would only ask you to do something if I believed you could do it," he said. "Just try and walk in her shoes. Meet her halfway."

"Have you asked Dawn to walk in my shoes?" I asked. "I just don't understand why I have to do all the walking!"

"Just try, Molly," he said. "Give it a chance."

I spent a few minutes in class trying to figure out how to make sense out of all of this. Shelly and Nellie wanted to be on our team. Jess supposedly wanted to play with Dawn's team. The Ballplayers and I had nothing to do with this fight, yet we were caught right in the middle. The adults didn't have a clue about what was going on. There was only one thing that was crystal clear: If things blew up, every one of them would be pointing at me.

Chapter Nine

After a unanimous vote, Penny, Rosie, Wil, and I agreed that no way in the world would we invite Shelly and Nellie to play on our team. We didn't even have to ask my mom or Rico. "They're bad news right now," Penny said. "And we don't need any more problems."

I thought about our team captain and wondered whether Dawn told her about Shelly and Nellie. "Let's not even tell Jess that they even talked to us," I said. "She might get mad at us for not asking her opinion."

"Who's going to tell Shelly and Nellie that we said no?" Rosie asked.

"I will," Penny said.

"Better you than me, P.," Wil added. "They wouldn't want to hear it if I gave them a piece of my mind."

Penny never gloated or whined about being the peacemaker. She had a knack for resolving situations without causing too much injury to either party. "I'll tell them that if we need more players, we'll let them know," she said.

"Sounds good," Wil said.

"Yeah," Rosie agreed. "They won't get mad at us."

I went home that day and rested a little easier. Before I went to bed, I practiced the splits a few more times. My mother pushed open the door and caught me as I was stuck in my weak attempt to reach a parallel position. "What in the world are you doing?"

"Working on my flexibility," I said. "Goalies need to be able to do the splits."

I grunted as I pushed myself down to the ground.

"It doesn't look like your body wants to bend that way," my mother said.

"I can do it!" I insisted even though I felt like my legs were breaking. I finished my last five seconds and then collapsed on the floor. I looked up at my mother sitting on my bed. I hadn't seen her since our early practice on Wednesday morning. She sat at the end of my bed, and Annie came over and curled up next to her. She asked about school and grades. I told her I was doing just fine.

"I know you're worried about the hockey team," she said.

For once we agreed.

"We're getting better, don't you think?" she asked.

I groaned and then covered my head with my pillow.

"I forgot to tell you," she said. "I invited some players to scrimmage against us at practice tomorrow."

I lifted the pillow off my face and asked, "Who?"

"Mike, Beef, Cowboy, and one more player," she said.

The Broadway Ballplayers

"Who?"

"Eddie," she said.

I hid my face underneath the pillow, cringed, and pleaded, "Why, Ma? Why?"

"He's not a bad kid," she said.

"Yes, he is," I said defensively. "You don't have to go to school with him every day. Then you'd see what he's really like."

"Well, he's coming tomorrow," she said. Then she tucked Annie in, gave us a kiss good night, and shut off the light.

When Eddie, Beef Potato, Cowboy, and the rest of the crew walked through the doors at six A.M. Friday, all of us stopped and turned their way. Eddie pulled off his long stocking cap. Beef Potato, who had made guest appearances on Broadway Ave., yelled out, "Would somebody put on the air-conditioning please? 'Cause I'm going to be burning up out there."

Cowboy grinned at all of us and said, "We heard you needed some hockey lessons."

"Who invited them?" Wil asked.

"I did," my mom said proudly. "We're scrimmaging today to get ready for the game."

"Let's go, Broadway!" Rico called out. "Back to our drills."

J. J. waved to all of his boys and then returned to his forward position. Jess lined up across from him and they broke into a two-on-one drill. It was them against me. I held my spot in the goal and kept my eye on the puck. Jess swung the stick back and *smack!* I blocked it.

110

"Yes!" Penny screamed. "Nice job, Z.!"

Z stood for Zamboni and that was my nickname for sweeping the ice. Penny and Rosie raced down the ice. I sucked air in and out waiting for their attack. Rosie closed in on me and faked the pass. *Smack!* I reached out and knocked down the puck again.

"You go, Z.!" Wil said. "You go!"

I tried to hide my grin, but it was impossible. For the first time in what seemed like an eternity, I had a rush of confidence. My teammates smiled as they bent down low and zipped around the rink. When the boys took the ice, I was sure this would be our turning point. I cheered for Jess during warm-ups. She was the one player who would lead us out of the basement and up to the first floor with everyone else in the league.

"Go, Broadway! Go, Broadway!" Wil chanted.

Eddie and Jess lined up for the face-off. When Rico dropped the puck, Jess got her stick on it and passed it to Penny. Penny advanced down the ice and then hit J. J., who was open on the left side. *Go, J. J.! Go!* Cowboy rushed out on him, and J. J. slipped right on by. He brought his stick back and snapped his wrists forward. *This is it! Yes!*

Beef Potato leaned to the right of the goal and knocked the puck down. All the boys cheered. J. J. screamed in frustration. I collapsed on the ice. "We were so close," I said. "So close!"

Unfortunately that was one of the few highlights for the Broadway Ballplayers. Eddie and Cowboy charged down the ice and made Wil, Anita, and me look as if we were ghosts. They scored two goals in a row. After Eddie scored the second, he snowplowed to a stop right in front of me and said, "How'd that feel?"

"Time out!" I screamed. I skated out to the middle of the rink and said, "Broadway, come here!"

One by one they skated up to me. I stared through the face masks of my friends. "I can't handle this anymore! Does anybody have any pride out here?"

They all gave me dirty looks and started muttering to each other.

"Do you think we like to lose?" Jess said.

"We're trying our best!" Wil added.

"Try harder!" I commanded. I handed all my goalie equipment to Wil and took the front line. I skated with Jess and Penny as they controlled the puck. Within thirty seconds, Jess scored. I yelled like a fool, then I stared at Eddie and said, "How's that one feel?"

Five minutes later our offense fell apart. I took it upon myself to barrel my way down the floor and force us into the goal area. After a bunch of shots, rebounds, and wild passes, the puck bounced off Eddie's skate and barely crossed the line.

"Yes!" Jess screamed.

"That was cheap," Cowboy said.

"We'll take it!" I said. I stood up on my toes and raised my stick above my head. When I locked my knees, I leaned too far and began to slip. I hit the ice like a ton of bricks, but without the crashing sound. My entire body throbbed. Penny tugged on my shoulder and pulled me up off the ice. "You're acting like we just won the national championship," she said. "The game's not over."

Scoring two goals was a team high for the season. All

I wanted was just one more. Instead of us controlling the game, Eddie's team took over. Actually, Eddie did all the work. He wiped away the devilish grin, skated with a serious look on his face, and dominated the ice. Nobody could touch him. I watched him in amazement and wondered if his mother or little sister had seen him play. I looked at the all-star jersey that was blowing in the wind and guessed that his teammates had all-star personalities to put up with a kid like Eddie.

During the next time out, I went back into the goalie position. When the game resumed, the attack headed my way. I squatted down and deflected one shot and then another. Eddie scooped up the rebound and fired a third time. The puck slipped between my skates. I threw myself on the ground and punched the ice.

"Nice try!" my mom yelled. "Hang in there, Molly!"

I cheered like crazy for the offense, hoping they would make up for my mistake. But they couldn't control the puck. Cowboy and Eddie attacked again.

"Come on, defense!" I screamed. "Stop 'em!"

Eddie made a sweet pass to Beef Potato, who had come out of the goal and planted himself right in the middle of the ice. Beef gently took the pass, skated two steps, and then, *whoosh!* The puck flew right by me.

When the game finally ended, I couldn't even look my teammates in the eye. The person who told them to play with pride was the one who stunk up the rink.

Sunday morning we received another thumping. My basketball friend Sheila and the Rockford Rockets put on another hockey clinic for us and we lost 5–2. During the game, Angel had to sit out because of her foot injuries, and then Wil bumped her knee on the ice. We finished with six players. Rico and my mom called us in for the huddle.

"I know you can't see it," he said. "But we're moving ahead. Sometimes for every one step forward, you have to take two steps back."

"Hang in, there!" my mom called out. "Keep your heads up!"

Jess didn't speak to anyone. She took her gear and walked out the front door. As I left the bench, I spotted Sheila taking off her goalie equipment.

"Nice game, Red," she said to me.

I rolled my eyes.

"Sorry," Sheila muttered. "I never know what to say."

"That's okay," I said, quickly forgiving her. "I didn't know you were playing."

"The rest of my teammates are on all these traveling teams," she told me. "I'm just in it for fun."

"You played a great game," I said. Sheila wiped away the sweat from her brow and then took a big sip out of her water bottle. The rest of my team came over and said hello.

"How long have you all played?" she asked.

"This is our first year," I answered.

"We haven't even come close to winning yet," Wil added.

"We pretty much stink," J. J. said bluntly.

I punched him in the arm. "Don't talk like that!"

"You need to get more players," Sheila suggested. "You all got tired. That's why we won."

All my friends stared at me and I looked back at them. Running back to Shelly and Nellie wouldn't be possible. Aside from knowing all the trouble they could cause, we didn't even know if they knew how to play. There had to be someone else.

"Why don't we just ask Eddie to play?" Angel suggested.

My mouth dropped open and I shook my head. "No," I insisted. "No way."

"You saw how good he is," Angel continued. "He could really help us."

"Yeah," J. J. said. "And I can use another guy around here."

Wil stared at the ground silently. I knew that she considered Eddie her biggest nightmare. Putting him on the team would be like forgiving him for all the bad things he did to torture all of us.

"I think he should play," Penny said.

"Me, too," Jess added. "There are only two more games left."

I turned back to Wil. She glanced up at me and muttered, "If he even starts acting like a fool, I'm gonna quit."

I huffed. As far as strategy, letting Eddie play was the right thing to help our team. But morally it was wrong. "I need some time to think about it," I said.

"I'm the captain," Jess pointed out.

I scoffed. "You're not the one who loses sleep over all of this."

"We need to ask the coaches before we do anything," Penny said.

"I'll talk to my mom about it," I said.

From across the rink my mother called out for all of us to hurry up.

"Why?" I yelled back.

"Who wants to go watch the Sharks play?" she asked.

If we had won, I would have been running out the door. "I don't think I can deal with Dawn right now," I said.

"Who's Dawn?" Sheila asked.

"It's a long story," Wil started to explain.

"Let's just go," Penny said. "See you later, Sheila!"

We all gave Sheila a high five, ran out the door, and hopped in our minivan. I hoped that we could slip into the rink without anyone spotting us. I didn't want Dawn to see us scouting her team. If she did, I knew she'd think we were scared.

When we arrived at the rink, no one looked our way. All eyes were on the ice. We settled in our cold seats and watched as the best hockey team in the city took the ice. All of the Sharks stood big and tall. Their skates smoothly scraped the ice. The puck looked like a magnet at the foot of their sticks. Dawn moved in synch with the rest of her teammates. None of them smiled. Nobody laughed. I took a closer look at Dawn and watched her frown. As the other players moved through the drills, they quietly encouraged the others. No one said anything to Dawn, nor did she speak or cheer for anyone else.

"She looks scared out there," Wil said. "Doesn't she?"

"She looks a lot smaller than she does at school," Penny pointed out.

I sat watching quietly. Dawn took a drink of water and sat down at the end of the bench by herself. Her coach spoke to each player one at a time, but he said nothing to Dawn. When the whistle blew, all the starters took the ice. Dawn stayed in her lonely spot at the end of the bench.

"Something's not right," I said. "That isn't the same Dawn we know."

"Didn't you hear?" a voice called out behind us.

We all turned and looked at a man who wore a big hockey jersey with SHARKS written across it.

"Dawn's been skipping practice a lot," he said. "The coach has been all over her about it. From what I hear, she's having some problems at school."

Nobody said anything. We all just turned back to the ice and pretended like we had no idea what the man was talking about. "It's strange," he added. "She seems like a really nice girl."

What? Are you crazy? I looked at Penny in disbelief. She just shrugged. Dawn had her teammates and fans fooled.

The Sharks went on to win the game 8–1. At the end, we all summed up what we had just witnessed.

"Maybe they're a little bigger and stronger than most teams," Angel said. "But that's all right. We can still win."

"Yeah," Penny said. "Every team can be beat."

"That's right," my mom cheered.

"We just have to hope that they're playing really bad and we're playing like All-Americans," Wil explained. "It's possible. Right, Molly?"

I shook my head a little bit and blinked a few times to snap out of my daze. I finally took my eyes off Dawn Miller and looked at my friends.

"Yeah," I said. "We can win."

Instead of just going back home and resting my body, my mother dropped off all of my friends and then started driving the other way.

"Where are we going?" I asked.

"To church," she said.

"I thought we weren't going today."

"We always go."

I huffed.

"I just want to go home and go back to bed," I said.

My mother ignored me and kept driving. Before we pulled into the church parking lot, I mentioned to my mother that we were thinking of adding another player to the team.

"Who?" she asked.

"We're still recruiting," I said. "We're looking for the player who can fit in with our whole team concept."

I grinned as my mom laughed. "You're looking for somebody who can win!" she said.

"I tried to say it the way adults do," I said. "Wil told me to talk like that. But you're right, Ma. I want to win one. Just one."

"Me, too, Molly," she said with a sigh.

My frozen toes thawed out while I sat in church later that morning. For the first twenty minutes, I thought about Eddie. I knew letting him play and giving him a chance was the right thing to do. But I had given Eddie so many chances before. *What if he comes along and messes things up? What if he hurts Wil's feelings again and starts being a jerk?* I couldn't come up with a solution, so I decided to sleep on it.

Ice Cold by Molly

I spent the remaining twenty minutes thinking about Dawn. I kept seeing how small she looked out on the ice when she was surrounded by the rest of the Sharks. She kept fidgeting and looking around begging for approval. She tried so hard on every drill and then stared at the ice when she didn't do exactly as her teammates expected. The weird thing was that I wasn't glad to see her suffering. I didn't grin when the man behind us told her how much trouble she was in. He thought she was a good kid. He felt bad for her. Never in my life would I have imagined Dawn Miller hitting rock bottom.

Chapter Ten

I walked down the hallway with my friends in school when Wil stopped in her tracks and said, "Look!" I looked up and spotted Shelly and Nellie stuffing books, notebooks, folders, and pens in their bags.

"Are you leaving school?" Penny asked.

"No!" Nellie's voice boomed.

"What's up?" Wil asked.

"It's none of your business what we're doing!" Nellie snapped.

"Sor-ry," Penny mumbled.

"Are you changing lockers?" Wil persisted.

They ignored us, which we took for a yes.

"Can you at least give us a hint?" Wil asked.

They shook their heads and grunted as they tried to squeeze all the books inside.

"Where's Dawn?" I asked.

"Who cares about her?" Nellie said.

It looked like we had hit the problem right on the head.

"I really think you need to get this out in the open," Wil said. "You're lookin' kind of stressed."

Shelly dropped a full folder and groaned as the loose paper scattered all over the floor. "All right, yeah. So?" she blurted out. "Maybe we are a little upset. Wouldn't you be if your best friend copied your homework, stole your boyfriend, talked behind your back, and lied about everything all the time?"

My mouth dropped open. I couldn't speak. Hearing the truth from these two girls was unbelievable. All of my friends stood stunned for a few seconds, and then finally Penny spoke. "What are you going to do about it?" she asked.

"We're moving our lockers down there!" Shelly squeaked.

"With us?" I blurted out.

"Yeah," she said.

I looked around at my friends in shock. Then Dawn Miller turned the corner. Her mean glare and clenched fists made it clear that she was going to blow. "You're not leaving!" she shouted. "*I'm* leaving!"

She pulled open her locker and started throwing all of her stuff on the floor. All three of them started screaming at each other. Faces flushed red. Eyes turned glassy. Penny grabbed on to Nellie's arm and said, "Relax." Shelly started yelling louder.

"You're such a liar!" she said.

Dawn spotted Shelly's pile of books and papers. She extended her foot and kicked them over.

"You're such a—" I gasped.

121

"Girls!" Mr. Gordon yelled over the noise. "In my office now! All of you! Right now!"

Yes! After all this time Dawn, Shelly, and Nellie would roast in the office. No longer could they weasel their way out. They had turned on each other, and now they were all going down. As they moped away, the Ballplayers and I walked toward our lockers.

"The office is the other way, girls," Mr. Gordon said. "Let's go."

I spun around and saw his eyes were looking our way. "Us?" I asked.

"Yes," he replied.

"We didn't do anything," Wil pleaded.

"In the office, now!" he repeated.

I threw my arms up in the air. Tears started to well in my eyes. "This is all because of me!" I said. "You always think I'm getting in trouble with Dawn. This isn't fair! We just walked down the hallway."

He reached his long arms around all of us and directed us down the hallway. We marched into the conference room and all quietly picked a seat around the oval table. I dropped down in my chair and huffed. The thought of being in the office with Dawn made me too weak to even look up.

"Can I just say something?" Wil pleaded.

"No," Mr. Gordon said as he sat at the head of the table. "Sit down, Wil."

"I just wanted—"

"Have a seat!" Mr. Gordon boomed.

Wil sank down in her seat and we waited. All of us liked Mr. Gordon, even though he threw the rule book at all of us on anything from not sitting up straight to flunking a test. He twiddled his thumbs and took a brief look at all of us.

"I'm tired of this, girls," he said. "Really tired. One at a time I'm going to ask you to speak and explain the situation. Penny, you begin."

Before Penny had a chance to say anything, Dawn blurted out, "She always gets to do everything first!"

"Be quiet!" I snapped.

"Hold it!" Mr. G. sounded more serious than I had ever heard before. My heart skipped a beat. "No one is allowed to speak unless you are spoken to first. If you talk out of turn, you will be suspended."

No one moved. "Penny," Mr. G. said. "Please continue."

"We were just walking down the hall and we asked Shelly and Nellie what was going on. They said they were switching lockers and that they didn't like Dawn anymore. We didn't do anything."

"Let me say this," Mr. Gordon commented. "I'd appreciate if you all got rid of the *we*. It implies that there are two sides here, and believe me, there will be only one side by the time we're finished. Nellie, please give me your version."

"We just wanted to switch lockers because Dawn is ruining our lives," she said. "I can't take it anymore, Mr. G. I just can't take it!"

I hid my grin, but inside I was thanking Nellie for explaining to Mr. G. that there weren't two opposing sides. It was all of us against one single person.

"Dawn?" Mr. Gordon asked.

Dawn scoffed. "They're all against me! You won't believe anything I say."

"Try me," Mr. G. said patiently.

"Jess was supposed to play on my hockey team, but Molly stole her from me. Then Shelly and Nellie said that Molly wanted them to play on her team, too."

I gasped for air. Just before I was going to unload, Wil elbowed me and shook her head. Then she pressed her finger against her lips and raised her eyebrows.

"Wil?" Mr. G. asked.

"You want the truth?" Wil said.

He nodded.

"All right," she said. "I'll break it down for you, Mr. G. It goes something like this: Either Dawn is lying like crazy or she's been misinformed. First, we didn't steal Jess from anybody. Second, none of us asked Shelly and Nellie to be on our team. They asked us."

Mr. G. then turned to Rosie. "Do you have anything to say?"

She shook her head.

"You sure?" he asked again. "This is your chance."

Come on, Rosie! Tell him! Speak up! Defend us! We're the Ballplayers! We're your friends!

"Are you calling our parents?" she asked. We all knew how Rosie didn't like school and how much trouble she got in when she brought home bad reports or teachers called.

"I'm not sure yet," he replied.

"Wil's story is my story," Rosie said surely. "We don't go around stealing players from anybody."

I grinned.

"Rosie, Wil, and Penny," Mr. G. said. "You're allowed to go. Any more problems, and you're in detention for the whole month."

My friends shrugged as they walked out of the room and left me all by myself.

"Sorry," Wil whispered. I hung my head feeling so alone.

After they left, Mr. G. told Nellie and Shelly to clean up their mess in the hallway and to return to their original lockers. "You both will be mopping the gym floor and picking gum off chairs in detention today," he added. "And we will have a private meeting later."

When they left the room, the air grew thick and tense. I couldn't imagine what was in store for me now. I peeked up at Dawn and caught her staring at the table. I stared at her waiting for her to look back at me, but she didn't. She gripped the arms of her chair firmly and began to rock. She sucked in air and held her breath.

"You two will meet in my office at eight tomorrow morning to discuss a solution to your differences," Mr. Gordon said. "I want you to put some thought into how you can help the situation. And you are not allowed to even think of dictating to the other person what she must do. I want you to take a look at yourself first. Understood?"

Neither of us said or did anything. "Is this clear?" he added.

We both nodded.

"You're dismissed."

Later in the day I explained the situation to the Ballplayers.

"What are you going to say?" Wil asked.

"Nothing," I said, "because it's all her fault."

"I think you'd better think of something else," Penny said. "'Cause that's not going to fly with Mr. G."

"She's the problem!" I pleaded.

"You don't have to tell us," Rosie said.

"But it's all in your approach, Mo," Wil added. "All in the approach."

None of my friends seemed willing to write out a script as to what I should say, so I thought it might be best if we just forgot about Dawn.

"Who wants to go to the park after?" I asked.

"It's cold and rainy," Rosie said.

"I've got a lot of homework," Wil said.

I looked at them in disbelief. "We're supposed to be the Ballplayers," I said. "This is our park!"

"Don't even try the guilt trip," Penny said. "I get up before my grandmother to play hockey four times a week."

"'Nuff said," Wil agreed.

I begged for a few more minutes, but my friends wouldn't budge. I went home and finished what little homework I had right after school. With Kevin home to watch Frankie and Annie, I wanted to get out for a while. I needed to clear some things in my head, and there was no better way than going to shoot hoops. But when I looked out the window and saw the rain coming down, I knew people in the neighborhood would give me a hard time if I was out shooting in a cold winter shower. I went out to the garage and picked up my skates and stick.

"Where are you going?" Annie asked.

"To the rink," I said.

"It's raining."

"No kidding," I replied. "I'm going to take an umbrella and ride the bus."

"Can I go?" she asked.

"No."

"Why not?"

"Because it's too cold for you," I said.

"That's not fair!"

"I'll be home in an hour or so," I explained. "I just want to practice for a little while."

After running through the rain and sitting in a smelly bus, I made it to the rink. I looked out on the ice and didn't find any friends or classmates. It felt good to be alone. I sat down on the bench and slipped off my sneakers. I stood up to hang my coat and turned toward the boys' room. Eddie Thompson walked out the door and headed for the rink. I looked up again at the creep and he stared back at me. Then we both nervously turned away. Out of the corner of my eye I watched as he took the ice, and *seriously* thought about leaving. But it was too late. I tightened up my skates and then *snap!* The top buckle broke and the lace ripped.

"Ugh!" I yelled.

It was all Eddie's fault. He made me mad and I pulled too hard on my skate. I held the broken buckle in my hand and tried to figure out what I could do to replace it.

"I've got some tape in my bag," a voice said.

I looked up at Eddie as he stood leaning against the wooden wall. He spoke softly. I waited for him to snicker, but he didn't.

"You want me to go get it?" he asked.

I hesitated, not knowing what I was getting myself into. Would Eddie really help me?

"Do you want it or not?" he asked.

"Yeah, I guess," I said, shrugging.

Eddie skated off and headed to the lockers. I bent

over and pretended like I was working on my skate, wondering when the real Eddie would show up.

"Here," he said as he stood in front of me. I reached up and took the tape.

"The lace and the buckle are broken," I explained.

Eddie bent over and took a close look at my skate. I waited for him to say something mean about my dirty old figure skates. "You need a new pair," he said. "You can't play hockey in these."

"I don't have any hockey skates," I said quietly. There was a little shame in my voice, but for some reason, I felt like it was okay to say what I did in front of Eddie. I knew that he, like most of us on Broadway, didn't have a lot of money to go throwing into fancy, new sports equipment. "Where'd you get your skates?"

"Our team has a sponsor," he said.

I jumped in my seat as he grabbed my foot.

"Hold still," he said. He pulled out a long strip of tape and told me to hold the other end while he ripped it. "This will work for now," he said. "But not for long."

I looked around, frantically hoping that no one would witness Eddie Thompson bent down on one knee in front of me. There would be no way to explain this to my friends or family.

"You want to pass the puck around?" he asked as he stood up.

I scanned the rink to see if any of his friends were there. I didn't recognize anyone. "You alone?" I asked.

He nodded. "I just like to skate sometimes."

We went out on the ice, and I made a conscious effort to be smooth and steady. I watched the way Eddie sprinted, stopped, and changed direction. The puck landed softly against the foot of his stick. He led me with a wild pass and I missed the puck.

"Bad pass," he said. "Sorry."

It was strange being so civil to each other. We didn't speak too much. I couldn't look at him. It felt like a weird dream. I wondered how much he came to the rink or played sports by himself. Maybe he played so much to get out of the house. I remembered what other kids said about Eddie's mother: "She's a witch." If any of it was even close to being true, he must have hated being home. But what about his little sister? Was his mother mean to her, too? Did they know how good he was at hockey? Did his mom even care?

All of my questions went unasked and unanswered. After about twenty minutes of skating, Eddie said he had to go.

"I have an extra pair of old hockey skates that should fit you," Eddie said. "Do you want me to drop them off at your house?"

I hesitated. An exchange might make us friends and I wasn't sure I was ready for that. "Whatever you want to do," I said casually. "You don't have to give them to me if you don't want to."

Eddie snapped back, "If you don't want them, I won't give them to you."

Nerves tingled up my spine. I knew I had said the wrong thing. "Whatever," I said and threw my hands up in the air.

Eddie turned and walked away.

After staying up late tossing and turning over both Dawn and Eddie, I hoped that I would sleep late the next morning. When I woke up at hockey practice time, I tried to snooze back to dreamland but had no luck. I looked at the clock and realized that I had less than four hours before I would have to face reality. I jumped up and went out to the kitchen. My mother looked up from the newspaper and greeted me.

"I can't sleep," I moaned.

"What's wrong?" she asked.

"It's from getting up so early for hockey," I said.

"Is that all?" my mother asked.

By her tone I could tell that she was waiting for me to volunteer personal information. I stared aimlessly into the refrigerator. "That's all," I said.

"Are you sure?" she insisted.

Mr. Gordon must have called and told my parents about my big meeting. I slammed the door shut and huffed. "Why is this such a big deal?" I said, raising my tone. "Eddie and Dawn are the biggest troublemakers around, and I'm the one who has to say I'm sorry? I don't get it."

"Just think about what Mr. Gordon asked you to do," she said.

"Walk in their shoes?" I blurted out. "I've already tried that. It doesn't work."

My mother sighed and shook her head. "You'd better come up with something fast," she said. "Mr. Gordon is not happy about this at all, and neither am I."

"What am I supposed to do?" I asked.

"I'd sit down and make a list of things you can do to help the situation."

"Like what?" I shot back.

"That's for you to figure out on your own," she said as

Ice Cold by Molly

she grabbed a piece of paper and a pen off the desk. "Here," she added. "I'll make you some French toast while you work."

I sat down at the table and stared at the blank sheet. I thought about a title. "How to Bully-Bust Lincoln School by Molly O'Malley."

"Remember that this is about your behavior, first," my mother reminded me.

I changed the title and started my list:

Things about me that Dawn doesn't like:

1. I'm mouthy. When Dawn says something, I tell her off.
2. I don't like to listen to how good she says she is. Who cares how great she thinks she is?
3. I get super mad when she picks on people who don't stand up for themselves. She picks a fight with anyone, I finish it. Somebody has to.
4. I hate to lose and she always loves to rub it in when I do. I really hate that.

My mother asked permission to read my list, and I said yes. She nodded her head as she read and then asked, "Do you mind if I add something?"

"I don't care," I said with an attitude. My mother scribbled something down. When she was finished, I slapped my hand down on the piece of paper and picked it up.

5. I am a good person who is afraid to show Dawn what a good friend and person I can be.

131

"A friend? Afraid?" I said defensively. "How can you say that?"

My mother ignored my plea and simply said, "Now list five things that you can do to change those things you wrote."

"Like what?" I asked. "I need an example."

"Well, in number one, you say you're mouthy. Write down that you will at least take a few seconds to settle down when you get upset. Those few seconds can make a big difference."

As I started writing, I mumbled, "This is so stupid."

1. I will take a few seconds to settle down. No more than seven.
2. I will pretend to listen to how good Dawn says she is, but I won't let it get to me. I'm better at basketball than she is anyway.

"What do I do when she picks on other people?" I asked my mom.

"Try and encourage others to stand up for themselves so you don't get into trouble," she said. "Dawn will stop picking on the kids who stand up to her."

While I thought about how Billy stood up to Dawn, I wasn't sure if that would prevent her from attacking again.

"One more thing," my mom added.

"What?" I said.

"Mind your own business when possible," she added. "Write it down."

I sighed in frustration. "Why am I doing this?" I mumbled as I wrote. "This is a waste of time."

3. Encourage kids to not put up with Dawn. Maybe think of starting a self-defense class.

Number three led me straight to number four, which was my most sensitive area.

4. Still try to win. If we don't, walk away before crying. Cry later at home. Alone.

I read number four aloud and my mom smiled.

"What about number five?" my mom said.

"You wrote it," I said. "How about you finish it?"

"Okay," she agreed. "Write this down."

I held my pen and waited.

"I will show Dawn what a good person I can be," my mom said slowly and deliberately.

I finished the sentence and set down my pen. "Repeat it aloud," my mother said.

"Do I have to?"

"Yes," she said.

"This is stupid," I argued.

My mother stared me down and waited. I picked up my paper and read:

5. I will show Dawn what a good person I can be. Win Miss Personality contest this year.

"Now take that list to school and look at it when you're at your meeting with Dawn."

I thought of how corny it would be to pull out a list in front of her and how much trouble my smart-aleck comments would get me into. But to make my mother happy, I folded up the paper and stuck it in my bag.

"I just can't figure her out," I said. "Maybe she has problems at home or somebody did something bad to her once. But that still doesn't give her the right to—"

"And it doesn't give you the right to judge," my mother said as she went to take out the garbage. "Whether or not you can figure Dawn out is not the point. It's how you deal with the situation. That's the test."

My mother disappeared out the back door. When she returned, she called out my name. I looked up as she held a pair of black hockey skates in her hand.

"Whose are these?" she asked.

I froze in disbelief. "They're for me," I said slowly.

"They're pretty nice," she said. "Who gave them to you?"

A chill shot up my spine. My mom didn't really have to know that Eddie and I actually got along. She wouldn't believe me even if I told her. No one would.

"One of the Ballplayers must have dropped them off for me," I said.

I grabbed the skates and hurried out of the kitchen before she asked any more questions.

Chapter Eleven

I reported to Mr. Gordon's office five minutes early. He sat me down in the conference room and said, "Your friend should be here any minute."

I sat upright in my seat. My palms began to sweat, and I started to tap my foot on the floor. *Relax!* I took a deep breath and leaned back in my chair. I pulled a book out of my bag and opened it. I crossed my legs and held my head in my hand as I pretended to read. Nothing stuck, so I started peeking at the clock. *She's late.* The door creaked open. Without looking at Dawn or Mr. Gordon, I picked up my book and tucked it back into my bag.

"I'll be in my office," Mr. Gordon said before he turned to leave us in the room. Alone.

The door clicked shut. I looked around the conference room and wondered if our school principal had any hidden tape-recording devices. Dawn fell into the seat two chairs away from me. I stared at the floor and did not speak. I listened to the hum of the clock. *I'm not talking until she does!* Two minutes of silence passed. I twisted in my seat and I lost all patience. I looked right at my enemy and a chill shot up my spine. I expected to see an angry scowl and a mean glare. When I saw glassy tears cover Dawn's baggy eyes, my heart skipped a beat. She sucked in a breath, held it, and then burst into tears. My mouth dropped open as Dawn held her head in her hands and cried like a baby.

"This is so stupid," she said as she wiped her face with the back of her sleeve. "I'm leaving."

My mind raced through my list. I had put time and deep thought into our meeting. There was no way she was jumping ship without some kind of explanation. "Wait!" I said.

"Why?" she asked. "Why are we even here?" She remained in her seat. We both knew that stepping outside of the room with a red face and teary eyes would not look cool at all. I waited for her to take a deep breath and then made my move.

"Look, Dawn," I said. "I don't like to fight with you. Do you like to fight with me?"

"No," she said. "But you make me so mad sometimes! You're always yelling at me and getting the other kids to not like me. You always tell Shelly and Nellie that they're dumb for hanging out with me."

She yelled all the time. She told other kids not to like me. She called me dumb and ugly and stupid.

"Everyone here is so annoying!" she added.

I threw my hands up in the air. "Time out!" I said. "I'm not going to sit here and tell you that I don't have a temper and that I'm nice and sweet all the time."

"No kidding," she shot back.

"Yeah, I have a temper and yeah, I don't like to lose," I went on.

"You *really* don't like to lose," Dawn corrected.

I could feel my face turn red. "I'm working on getting better about those things, all right! But what about you?"

"What about me?" she said. "You've got the whole school against me!"

"That's not true."

"Yeah, it is," she said. "You talked Jess into playing on your team when I wanted her on mine! That wasn't fair!"

I really wanted to pick up a book and throw it at her. *Patience, Molly! Patience! Count to seven.* "This isn't about Jess or anyone at school," I said.

"Then what's it about?" she scoffed.

"You and me," I said after a few seconds.

"You're the one who's always getting me in trouble," she said.

"Oh, yeah," I said. "I get it. I'm the one who makes you pick on Billy Flanigan and calls kids names?"

She didn't answer my question. "You're the one who always tells on me!"

The thought of being called a rat made me clench the arms of my chair. "Look, I know I'm no angel," I began. "And honestly, I get mad at myself when I'm mean."

"Well, maybe I do, too," she said.

"Sure doesn't seem like it," I told her.

137

"Well, how do you know? You're not me! I try to help people and be nice to them when you're not watching."

"Okay, fine," I blurted out. "So maybe that guy in the stands had a point."

"What guy?"

"A fan said you're a nice girl and your coach has been hard on you lately."

"Someone said that?"

I nodded.

She was speechless.

"Can we call it a day and say we both will work to be better people?" I suggested.

The words echoed in the quiet room. I couldn't believe I was having a conversation where I included Dawn Miller in the *we*. She sniffled and I walked across the room and grabbed a few tissues out of the box on a desk. I handed them to Dawn. She looked at my hand and then slowly raised hers. She wiped her tears.

"You want to get outta here?" I asked.

She nodded. "Yeah, but you go first. I need a few more minutes by myself."

I softly shut the conference room door and hustled down the short hallway. I waited for Mr. G. to call out my name, but I made it to the door without a sound. If he had asked me how it went, I'd have to tell him that Dawn cried and we agreed on being better people. No one would believe that story.

I turned the corner and saw Jess coming in my direction. She stopped in front of me with a frown.

"What's the matter?" I asked.

"You're going to be really mad at me," she said and looked away nervously.

"What?" I gasped.

"I can't play on your team anymore."

I shook my head in denial. The whole season flashed before my eyes. "What are you talking about?"

"I made the all-state team," she said. "They want me to travel with them."

"Can't you play both?" I asked.

"No," she said. "My mother said it would be too much."

A monitor called down the hallway for us to get to class.

"Sorry, Molly," Jess said as she walked away.

My heart fluttered. Just when I thought I was starting to control myself, tears welled in my eyes. I ducked into the bathroom to get my composure. Despite what had happened in that office, we still had to beat Dawn's team. Without Jess, we wouldn't have enough players. Without Jess, we wouldn't have a chance.

Chapter Twelve

How'd it go with Dawn?" Penny asked as she unloaded her books into her locker.

"All right."

"What do you mean, all right?" Wil asked.

I shrugged.

"Was anything thrown across the room?"

I shook my head.

"Did you fight?"

"No!" I said.

Obviously my friends were going to have a difficult time believing what happened to Dawn Miller when she was behind closed doors. "She started to cry," I said.

"Excuse me?" Wil asked.

I nodded. "Real tears."

"Are you kidding?" Penny called out.

"Nope."

"What did you say that made her cry?" Wil asked.

"Nothing," I said. "I just sat there and all of a sudden she's bawling. I couldn't believe it myself."

My friends stood wide-eyed. Wil kept shaking her head. "Has anyone ever seen Dawn cry?" she asked. "I didn't think that girl had tear ducts."

"Don't say anything," I said. "If we make a big deal of it, she'll start being the old Dawn again."

Penny smiled. "What's gotten into you?"

"What do you mean?"

"Why are you being so nice about this?" Wil asked.

"I'm not being nice," I said. "I still don't like her if that's what you're thinking."

No, I didn't tell them that I told Dawn that "we" would work on being better people. I didn't tell my friends that when she started yelling at me, I'd kept my cool. They would label me as "reformed" or "crazy," and I was neither.

"Forget about it," I said. "We've got bigger problems to talk about."

"What?" they all asked.

"Jess can't play with us anymore," I announced.

"No!" Wil shrieked.

"She shouldn't have quit on us." I said. I could feel my temperature rise.

"Why'd she quit?" Penny asked.

"She's playing on the state traveling team, and she says she can't do both."

Penny looked at me. "You know how badly she wanted to play with the state team."

Penny had a point, but I didn't care. "She's caused so many problems."

"Not really," Penny said. "We begged her to be on the team."

"I was just trying to do the right thing," I said. "She didn't have to play if she really didn't want to."

"It just didn't work out, Molly," Penny said. "Don't go getting mad at Jess over this. It really isn't her fault."

"Fine!" I said. "It's all my fault. It's always my fault!"

When I listened to what I had said, I scared myself. I sounded like Dawn as she whined in the principal's office.

"What are we going to do?" Rosie asked.

"I'll figure something out," I said. "It was my idea in the first place."

"Do you perform miracles?" Wil asked. "We're going to need one here."

"We're running out of players," Rosie pointed out.

"There's no one else left," Penny added.

I couldn't let my friends overpower me. "We're a team!" I said. "Let's stay together! We'll make it through this!"

"Oh, we'd better," Wil said. "Everybody at the rink is talking about how bad we are. They're talking about how we look like fools on the ice. I can't take this anymore."

When I turned to Penny and she said nothing to support me, my eyes started to water. "I'll take care of it!" I said as my voice cracked. I slammed my locker shut and ran down the hallway. I felt the tears run down my cheeks and ducked into the bathroom. I hid in the stall and wiped my tears with toilet paper.

"Molly," Penny's voice called out. "I'm sorry. I didn't mean to hurt your feelings."

"Well, you did!" I called out.

"I said I'm sorry."

I slowly pushed open the door and faced my best friend. "I'm sorry for getting mad and saying bad things about Jess," I said. "I'm a little stressed."

"I didn't notice," Penny said.

As we talked, Jen Lynn walked in the door. I said hi and then smiled as a thought occurred to me. "Hey, Jen," I said. "You still play hockey?"

She nodded. "Yeah, sometimes."

"You want to play on our team?" I asked, getting excited.

Jen asked about the details and I filled her in. She said she could make it to our game on Sunday. "Will anybody care that I haven't been to practice?"

Penny and I shook our heads. "Just promise us you'll be there," Penny said, and Jen nodded.

Later that night I told my mom and dad about how Jess was leaving the team and how I invited Jen to play. For a minute I wanted to complain about Jess pulling the rug out from under us, but I didn't. I told them that the Ballplayers were comfortable with the change in roster, and that I really believed that things would work out.

"That's great, but we're not worried about the team right now," my mother said. "I'm a bit more concerned with how the meeting between you and Dawn went this morning."

"Oh," I said. "I forgot about that already."

"Well, we didn't," my dad said. "Please fill us in."

"We sat there in complete silence for what seemed like forever. Then she started to cry," I said. "The amazing part was that I didn't do anything crazy. I just sat there even when she started yelling at me."

"Why do you think she cried?" my father asked.

"I don't know."

"Maybe she's a little more human than you thought," my mom suggested.

I didn't respond.

"So you're getting along now?" my dad asked.

"This doesn't mean I like her," I said defensively. "We're not friends."

My parents looked at each other and shook their heads. "She's stubborn like you," my mother said to my father. My father found it as amusing as I did—not very.

"What?" I said. "This doesn't have anything to do with being stubborn. I just don't like the girl and I have good reasons not to."

"You used to be friends with her," my mother reminded me.

"Well, that was a long time ago, back when she was nice."

"I'm sure she still can be a friend," my dad said.

I sighed. My parents were asking way too much. I didn't force them to be friends with people. This was crazy.

"I tried my best today," I pleaded. "I even told Dawn I thought she could be a good person. Isn't that enough?"

"For now," my mother said softly.

When Angel limped into the rink on Sunday morning, I knew that we would have to activate Jen Lynn immediately.

"I can't play," Angel said. "My doctor doesn't want me skating."

"It's all right," I assured her. "We're already hurting enough. We don't want any serious injuries."

"What is the team going to do?" she asked.

"We've recruited another player," I explained.

"Who?" Wil asked, surprised.

"Jen Lynn," I said.

"Does she know our record?" Wil asked.

"I forgot to tell her."

As we warmed up, I thought that maybe the Pueblo Panthers would fall into the trap of looking at our dismal record and not taking us seriously. We'd catch them playing at half-speed and then *BOOM!* We'd all play out of our minds and win 10–0! The Panthers wouldn't even know what hit 'em.

"Bring it in, Broadway!" Rico yelled.

I skated over and gave all my teammates a hard slap on the back.

"We can do this! Let's win!"

The Panthers came out focused and firing. After a few minutes, a stream of sweat ran down my back. I was screaming at everybody as I threw myself in front of the goal. I reached right and then dived left. "Help me! Somebody help me!" I barked. The puck slipped under my stick and between my legs for the score. "Ugghh!" I yelled.

Everybody tried to tell me to shake it off, but I couldn't. What burned me most was that I had let the easiest shot slip right by. From that point on, every shot was a matter of life and death. We held the Panthers scoreless for two periods. As we skated into the huddle, everyone slapped me on the back. "Way to play, Mo!" Penny said.

For once, we played some defense. But without Jess

we lacked the punch we needed on offense. I turned to J. J. He wiped his brow with a towel and then sucked down some water. "Could you pick it up on O.?" I asked.

"I feel like I'm playing for two people," he said. "There's not enough of us out there."

I felt a tap on my shoulder. I turned and looked at Wil. Her hair was sticking on end. Her glasses slipped down her nose. She sniffed and said in a weak voice, "I feel like I'm going to pass out."

A chill shot up my spine. Wil couldn't leave us now. We didn't have any more players. The game was close. We had a chance.

"I'm really sick, Molly," she insisted as she started to shiver.

"Mom!!" I called out. My mother came over and checked Wil out. I skated away knowing that I could not be objective at all. I didn't want my friend to make her illness worse, but I knew that I would be sick if we blew this game. I turned back to my mom as she sat down with Wil at the end of the bench. With one less body to stop the incoming pucks, I let two goals zoom past me. When the final buzzer sounded, I took off my helmet and threw it on the ice. My dad yelled from deep in the bleachers, "Molly!" I picked up my helmet and stormed off the ice.

"Keep your heads up!" Rico called out. He smiled. He patted us on the back. He had coached us through all the low lights. I started to feel bad for Rico and my mom. We couldn't even win for them.

"We need more players," J. J. said in the aftermath. "Can I ask one of my friends to play?"

"No," I said, knowing how annoying most of J. J.'s friends were.

"Why not?" he asked.

"Because we can't just go inviting random people to play on our team," I said.

Penny and J. J. looked over at Jen and then back to me. "Oh, really?" J. J. said.

"We all know who we need to ask," Penny said.

"No," I begged. "He'll ruin everything."

"What's there to ruin?" Anita asked.

"I'm not asking him," I repeated.

"Why do you have to be so stubborn?" J. J. asked. "We're one week away from playing against the Sharks. We're going to lose if you don't ask him. Do you *want* to lose?"

I stood silently as all my teammates waited for my decision.

"Let me sleep on it," I said.

Chapter Thirteen

As I sat in the pew during church later that day, I could still feel the sweat on my back from another terrible loss. I leaned over, took a whiff of myself, and winced. I smelled like a skunk.

"Peew!" Frankie said. "You stink!"

My face turned hot in embarrassment. I looked around nervously to see if anyone had heard or could smell me. Two older ladies behind me made eye contact and then looked away. I elbowed Frankie in the side. He yelped. My father turned toward me. His brow furrowed and he tightened his lips. I turned my attention to the front. For the first time in twenty minutes I listened to the priest.

Father Joseph stood in the middle of the altar. His voice carried softly over the crowd. I watched as he opened, closed, and folded his hands together. He pointed at the crowd slowly and deliberately and then touched his chest with his index finger.

"Seventy times seven," Father Joseph said. "That's as many times as you should forgive a person."

Then he stopped and stared directly at me. I dropped my head in shame. I clasped my hands together in my lap and started praying silently. I apologized to Dawn and Eddie and anybody else who couldn't hear me. I had a problem with the numbers seven and seventy, so I started with one. One more try for Eddie. And maybe if he appreciated my forgiveness, I'd come up with some special plan for Dawn as well.

I rushed through my homework and finished it all by one o'clock that afternoon. When my parents questioned the quality of my work, I simply pulled out my last three test scores, which were all A's. They signed my papers as I called the Ballplayers on the telephone. "See you at the park in ten minutes," I told them each of them.

My skin tightened as I jogged down to Broadway Avenue through the frigid winter wind. I skipped across the sandlot and stopped right under my favorite spot in the whole world: the basketball hoop. I pulled my gloves on tight with my teeth and looked up at the bent rim. I held the ball up high and started to shoot layups. The sound of the chain as the ball went through the net made me smile. I couldn't wait until the basketball season.

"It's too cold to shoot," Wil said as she walked over.

I rolled my eyes and said, "It's never too cold for basketball."

"Then it's too windy," Wil whined.

"I thought you were sick."

"I feel better now," she said. I was sure Wil's father was working and that she didn't even bother to tell her step-mom about how sick she felt in the morning. "Your mom said I could come over later for dinner," Wil told me. "She said she'd make some chicken soup for me."

"She'd be mad at you if she knew you were out in the cold right now," I said.

"Don't tell her. I just took a nap and now I need some freezing cold air to make me feel better. I read some-where that it's the best medicine."

I looked up and saw Penny jog over with a football cradled in her arm. Penny's thick hood flopped back and forth behind her head and the legs of her sweatpants swished together. She spun around and pointed at Rosie and Angel, who were walking not too far behind. "What up? What up?" Penny called out with a smile.

"This is perfect football weather," Wil said.

All of us gathered together for a quick chat. After a few minutes I began to feel the chill so I started dancing around in my spot. "We'd better play something before we all freeze," I said.

We started throwing the football around and covering each other for the long passes. Wil tried to sneak an inter-ception, but I beat her to the ball.

"We're in!" J. J. screamed as he came jogging across the frozen grass. Eddie strutted alongside J. J. I could see his breath in the cold air. While the rest of us were wrapped in hats and gloves and layers of sweatshirts, Eddie wore nothing on his hands or head. Mr. Tough

Guy always claimed he never got cold, but his tight red fists and bright red cheeks betrayed him.

"I'm not playing if Eddie's playing," Wil said. "You should have heard the things he was calling me yesterday."

Billy, Mike, and Sleepy joined us within minutes. Penny talked Wil into playing and then she split us up into two teams.

"Tackle," Eddie sneered.

"That's fine with me," I said, determined to be tough.

"No," Penny decided. "Every time we play tackle at least three people get hurt or we get into an argument. Two-hand touch."

"Fine," he said. "Let's play the girl game."

I scowled at Eddie. But before I unloaded on him, I thought about the skates he had left on my back porch. I gave him another dirty look and muttered, "You can be such a jerk."

"You girls are such wimps," Eddie said back.

That was it. Skates or not skates, I didn't care. "The girl comments are getting kind of old, don't ya think?"

Eddie looked at me and shook his head. "I was just kidding," he muttered. But it wasn't funny. I looked around and noticed no one had joined me in my protest. I waited for somebody to back me up by slinging some cheap shot at Eddie. No one did.

"Let's go," Penny said. "We'll kick off to you first."

I stormed over to one side of the field with my team. Penny threw the ball long and high into the air. Eddie took two steps in and waited for the ball to fall into his hands. I sprinted madly across the frozen ground with my eyes locked on Eddie. Penny and Rosie also closed in and steered Eddie in my direction. I reached out and firmly put two hands on him.

"Gotcha!" I yelled and I grinned. Eddie said nothing. He just dropped the ball down and retreated to his team's huddle. I walked back to mine wondering why he didn't snap back at me. But after running the next few plays, I forgot about Eddie being such a pain and just played the game.

Surprisingly, we made it through without any major injuries or wrestling matches. I caught three passes in our victory over Eddie's team. I even intercepted a pass right before it fell into Eddie's hands. After the game Eddie picked up my basketball, walked over to the courts, and started shooting. "He could have asked to use it," I said to Penny. She didn't respond. "Don't you think he could have asked?" I repeated louder.

"Yeah," Penny said. "But that's Eddie just being Eddie."

The wind grew fierce and the crowd began to clear. I said goodbye to my friends. Wil said that after finishing her homework and taking another catnap, she'd be over for dinner. As they left, I turned and watched as Eddie kept shooting. The tips of his ears were bright pink. His hands looked blue.

"You need your ball?" he asked.

I wanted to say yes just because I wasn't too comfortable with his hands on my favorite object in the entire world. I paused, knowing the right thing to do especially on a Sunday would be to share. "You can use it if you want," I replied.

"I'm not going home for a while," he muttered.

I could feel the hurt in his words. His eyes looked on

the ground and then up to the hoop. He did not say anything else. Something must have happened. "Why not?" I asked.

"I don't want to," he said. "No reason."

I rebounded a few of his shots, and then he passed the ball to me after he missed.

"How's Dawn?" he asked. I looked carefully at him and noticed a trace of a grin. He must have heard about our meeting in the principal's office.

"Why do you care?" I said defensively.

He scoffed. "I was just asking. I know how she is."

My mouth dropped open. *You know how she is?* The thought of Eddie talking to me about Dawn and her infamous personality was absurd.

"She tries to act tough all the time," he said. "But she's really not."

I lost all concentration and bricked my next shot. I couldn't believe what Eddie was saying about Dawn. Did he see himself as anything like her? Did he think he had to act tough all the time?

Eddie passed the ball back to me and mumbled, "Keep shooting." He rebounded for me and then we took turns for a few more minutes. As the time passed, I started to feel more guilty about not giving Eddie a chance.

A few minutes later I told Eddie I had to go home for dinner. Eddie passed me the ball. I caught the cold ball and tucked it under my arm. As I walked off, I felt a sudden urge to do something so unlike me. I spun around and asked, "Hey, Eddie, you busy on Wednesday, Friday, or Sunday mornings?"

He shook his head.

"Do you want to play on our hockey team for our last game?"

He blinked twice, then shrugged and said, "Yeah. I guess."

"Do me a favor," I said.

"What?" he asked.

"Don't pick on Wil."

He scoffed and glared at me.

"I mean, please don't pick on Wil," I repeated, more carefully.

"All right, fine," he said defensively.

"And no more girl comments," I added. "You're out-numbered and we've got the power to release you at any moment."

"Ha, ha," he said.

"I'm not kidding," I said as I walked away. "See you at practice."

I passed J. J. on my way home as he walked down to meet Eddie.

"You're not alone anymore," I told J. J.

"Say what?" he asked.

"I asked Eddie to play on our team," I replied.

J. J.'s eyes widened and he smiled a big, loopy grin. "You did?"

I nodded.

"What'd he say?"

"Of course he said yes," I said. "Would you pass up a chance to play with a team like ours?"

J. J. rolled his eyes. "I wouldn't go that far." He looked in the distance and pointed at Eddie. "Yeah, bro!" he yelled. Then he turned back to me and said, "Now instead of people pointing at me, they'll be talking about the both of us."

"I didn't know people were saying things," I said.

"Yeah," J. J. admitted. "It's rough being the only guy on the team."

I smiled, hoping J. J. was just joking.

"I'm serious," he said.

"And I still think it's funny," I said as I kept walking. With a laugh, I called out to the guys, "You're crazy to think I'm gonna feel sorry for you."

Eddie and I made it through two practices without any major confrontations. He left Wil alone and did what the coaches asked. But when we lost our scrimmage Friday morning, he returned to his old ways.

"I wish somebody on this team could pass," he sneered.

"We can," Wil shot back. "We just don't pass it to you because we'll never see the puck again."

"That's right," Eddie said. "'Cause I can do something with the puck unlike the rest of you sorry players."

I pushed off in the direction of Eddie Thompson. Just before I took my second step, a muscular arm grabbed me around my shoulder. I lost my balance and clung to the arm. I looked up and saw Rico holding me back.

"Enough!" Rico yelled. "Have a seat, Eddie!"

As the coaches reviewed a few plays and pointed out our weak spots, all I could think about was Eddie messing everything up and ruining our team. Neither he nor I would make it to seventy times seven. He was already close to failing at the first free break I had given him.

Five minutes later tempers cooled and the coaches had us huddle together in the middle.

"This is our last practice," Rico said. "And Sunday is our last game."

I had waited for what seemed like forever to get my revenge. The South Side Sharks were going down.

"Let's go out on Sunday and give it all you've got!" Rico added.

"Go out and have some fun!" my mom cheered.

I looked around at my teammates. Penny stared blankly ahead. Wil was still glaring at Eddie. Eddie tapped his stick on the ice. J. J. looked at the clock on the wall. Losing had stolen our spirit. No rah-rah cheers or pep talks could make a difference. The only thing that would end the pain and return us to our normal selves was one simple word that started with a *W*.

Win.

Chapter Fourteen

When we went to school that morning, Mr. Gordon pulled me aside and told my friends to go on to class. My face grew hot as they walked away with their eyebrows raised.

"Show me some hustle, please," Mr. G. called out to the Ballplayers. Their feet racewalked away and they didn't look back.

"What I'd do now, Mr. G.?" I blurted out. "I've been a good kid. Honest!"

"I know you have," he assured me. "I just wanted to check in to see what your secret was in the meeting you had with Dawn."

"I still don't like her," I snapped.

He stared up at the ceiling and shook his head.

"What?" I said. "It's the truth! She still annoys me. And we're playing her team on Sunday."

"So this is the big weekend," he said.

"Yeah," I replied. "If we lose, she'll be bragging to the whole school. I don't know if I'll be able to take it."

"Everything will be fine," Mr. G. said. "Trust me."

"You're dreaming if you think Dawn and I are going to be best friends after all of this," I told him.

He paused. I waited. "Do you realize how stubborn you can be?" Mr. G. stated.

I cringed, wondering if I could get some special permission for people not to say that word around me.

"What time is the big game on Sunday?" Mr. Gordon asked.

"Eight in the morning," I said.

"I heard that you added a player to your team this week," he said with a grin.

I looked into my principal's smile and didn't like it one bit.

"Our best player got moved up to the state team," I explained. "We were desperate. Really desperate."

"That was kind of you to ask Eddie," he said.

"Yeah, well," I said. "We need Eddie to win."

"I think it's a little more than that."

"Don't make this complicated, Mr. G.," I said. "It's a simple move to get a simple win."

"You're giving him a chance," Mr. G. said. "I'm proud of you."

For whatever reason, I wasn't very proud of myself for being so nice to the two biggest bullies in our school. I was playing with fire. At any given moment they could destroy everything and make me and so many other kids miserable again. The bell rang and Mr. G. rested his hand on my shoulder. "Keep walking in those shoes," he said.

"Whatever, Mr. G.," I said. "But how 'bout I just try walking to class for now?"

"Sounds good to me."

After my fourth class, I grabbed a sandwich out of my locker and headed toward the lunchroom. Billy and Paul ran up to me.

"I hope you beat the Sharks on Sunday," Billy said. "We're gonna be there."

"The whole school is," Paul added.

I said thank you and then took a spot in line. Shelly and Nellie strolled past me and sat at a new table with a new group of friends. Then Dawn came in and sat down at a table alone. She pretended to scratch something down on a sheet of paper. She had no food or drink. She just looked at her piece of paper and kept writing. I waited for somebody to sit down with her, but no one did. Shelly and Nellie stared at her from across the room and whispered things to each other. After I picked up my snack, I headed toward the Ballplayers, who were sitting at the table in the back of the room. My mind raced as I thought about passing Dawn's table. *I still don't like her! I won't ever forget what she's done to all of us.* But I took a closer look at her and saw how much smaller she seemed sitting all by herself. *Should I at least say hello?* After one more step Dawn looked up at me, jumped up from her seat, and bolted out of the cafeteria.

Chapter Fifteen

As we warmed up Sunday morning, I looked around the empty rink waiting for the doors to be pushed open and for all the kids from Lincoln School to pack the place. "Where is everybody?" I called out.

"Are you crazy?" Penny said. "Nobody wants to get out of bed this early on a Sunday morning."

Just at that moment Billy and Paul skipped through the doors. "We've got fans!" I cheered. Just as the words flew out of my mouth, I stopped and looked at the other end of the rink as Dawn Miller stepped onto the ice with the rest of her team. Out of the corner of my eye, I watched Dawn skate through a few drills and then return to her position. She looked so average next to the rest of the tall and strong Sharks.

"Shelly and Nellie said they're coming and cheering for us," Wil said.

I rolled my eyes. We didn't need any more trouble. "Let's just concentrate on the Sharks, all right?"

"Sor-ry," Wil added. "I forgot this is for the Stanley Cup."

All kidding aside, this game would go down in the history books at Lincoln School. J. J. and Eddie zipped through warm-up drills without punching each other or laughing. Penny, Rosie, and Anita did the same. Angel cheered from the sideline. My mother and Rico watched in silence.

The whistle blew and we skated in. "Don't let anybody score," Eddie said to me. I nodded my head even though he was asking a lot. I had heard about the Shark attacks for a month. From what everyone told me, I was going to have fits in the goal trying to stop the ambush. "Do me a favor," I said to my team as we huddled together for the last cheer. "Score a lot!"

All my teammates nodded.

"Let's give Dawn a workout!" Penny said.

"It's payback time!" Wil called out.

"No more losing," J. J. said. "It's a new season right now!"

I took my place in the goal and watched as Eddie took the face-off. Dawn crouched down in the cage opposite me. This was the makings of a bad dream: teaming up with one bully to beat another.

The referee dropped the puck and the game was underway. I jumped and twisted with every offensive move. I cringed on the turnovers and cheered on the smooth passes. Eddie, Penny, and J. J. did a solid job of keeping the pressure on Dawn's end of the ice. Then one huge Shark pushed J. J. out of the way and came right at me. One pass. Two pass. *Bam!* I blocked my first shot. A Shark got the rebound. *Bam!* I blocked the next. Wil crashed into a Shark as she slid the puck out of the middle. Then Anita swept a sweet pass up to Penny.

"Way to go, Broadway!" my mom cheered.

The momentum swung back and forth for the entire first period. Bodies thrashed everywhere. Skates, pads, and sticks slammed against the boards. Just before the second period began, we remained focused and quiet in the huddle. Everybody in the league knew that this period was when the Sharks loved to attack.

"We need a total team effort here," Rico told us. "Nobody relax!"

I looked around into the eyes of all of my teammates. Everybody was concentrating. Everybody was ready. "Win!" we cheered.

The Sharks coach put in his biggest and strongest lineup. I looked down at the goal cage and did not recognize the goalie. I stared over at the bench and saw Dawn sitting down. I didn't want her to be out of the game. I wanted her to be in. If we won and she didn't play, she'd say that it was because her coach didn't play her. *Come on! Put Dawn in!*

With or without Dawn, the Sharks' star players dominated the game. All their offensive plays and weapons clicked together at once. The referees let all the checking go. Even Eddie and J. J. couldn't keep up with the Sharks' swift passes. Penny fell three times. Rosie fought like a champion, but she couldn't out-muscle the faster and stronger players. I lost my breath trying to keep up with the shots. They scored one goal in the first three minutes. The second goal came one minute later. Then they scored two more in the last two minutes of the period.

I pleaded for help. My teammates assured me they were doing their best. After a while I fell into a state of shock and just kept my mouth shut. We were going down fast.

Midway through the third period, Eddie took an awesome shot on goal and scored. I cheered wildly. "Yes!" When I noticed that Dawn was the one in the goal, I jumped off the ice and actually landed on two blades. I froze when I noticed that the Sharks' coach was sending in the third-string goalie. Dawn skated off the ice with her chin down. Her coach got right up in Dawn's face and screamed, "When are you going to listen? When are you going to learn? Start focusing!"

I had never seen anyone yell at Dawn like that at school. I waited for Dawn to yell back or throw her stick at him, but she didn't. She simply returned to her spot on the bench and stared at the wall in front of her.

"Three more goals," Wil told me. "Do you believe in miracles?"

We both looked up and noticed the digital clock stop at three minutes and fifty-nine seconds. "There's still time left," I said.

"One goal every minute for the win," Wil calculated.

"We need to get the puck to Eddie," I said.

"I can't believe you just said that."

"Neither can I," I told her. "But it's our only chance."

Eddie got the puck on the next two possessions and scored each time. I had never seen him work so hard and so fast. All the other players on our team stayed out of his way and cheered him on. I wasn't embarrassed to say his name. I was cheering for Eddie Thompson. We all were.

"Go, Eddie, go!" Wil chanted.

With less than a minute left and the score 4–3, we all waited for Eddie to save our season. Penny and Rosie got control of the puck, but they couldn't find room to pass it to Eddie. He had two players on him at all times. He started calling for the pass and we tried, but nothing worked. I could see by the way his skates dug into the ice and how he gritted his teeth that Eddie wanted to win as badly as the rest of us.

But we didn't. When the final buzzer sounded, it felt like a punch in my stomach. I looked at the clock and wanted one more minute. I looked at the Sharks' coach as he yelled at all of his players. He had to be glad that the game was over. We lined up to shake hands, and of course, my insides collapsed and I started to cry. I kept my helmet on, hoping that no one would see my tears. I imagined Dawn Miller skating through that line with a grin on her face, fueling up before she said something to rub our loss and our entire season in my face. I refused to look at anyone on the other team, and I closed my ears to all their "good games."

After the game I went to the bench and sat by myself. I tried to wipe away my tears because I was afraid my friends would get mad at me for being such a baby and crying all the time. The more I tried to stop the tears, the faster they streamed down my face. My friends didn't even look at me. They knew I was bawling because I always did when we lost. I hated being such an emotional wreck over a sporting event. How embarrassing. I gave up the fight and stood up.

"Sorry for such a bad season," I said. "I'm sorry for it all."

A few people tried to say it was all right and not to worry about it. But I couldn't get over it. We went an entire season without one single win. It was all my fault.

Later in the locker room Penny came up to me and rested her arm around my shoulder. Then she backed off and said, "Pew! That goalie equipment really stinks. Have you washed any of that stuff? Or is it you, Mo?"

I shook my head and burst into laughter. After a minute I asked, "Do you get mad at me when I cry so much? Tell me the truth."

"No," she said. "I don't get mad. I know it's just because you care. Besides, you weren't the only one out there crying tonight."

I went through all of the players on our team and couldn't think of anyone I had seen in tears. "Who else was?"

"Dawn," Penny said.

"She was?" I asked.

Penny nodded. "Didn't you look at her going through the line?"

"She won! Why was she crying?"

"You saw how her coach screamed at her," Penny added. "And how she didn't talk to most of her teammates. It's no secret that the whole school has ganged up on her."

Penny stopped for a minute and then added, "Maybe Dawn didn't think she really won this time."

Chapter Sixteen

As my family walked in the house after church that day, I looked down at my brother's feet. "Frankie has my favorite sneakers on!" I waited for my mother and father to say something, but they were too far ahead of me. Or maybe they were just ignoring me.

"My shoes are too small and they hurt my feet," Frankie said.

I didn't buy it. "Take them off!"

Frankie started jumping up and down and running around in the garage. With every step and scuff, I gritted my teeth harder.

A little Larry the Lobster would do the trick for sure. But then my little sister and brother would go running around calling me a bully and my mom would be all over my back. I couldn't handle any more stress that day. I exhaled a huge breath and said with a phony smile, "Go ahead, wear them!" I walked into the house and shut the door.

"What was the problem out there?" my mother asked.

"Don't worry, Ma," I said. "I've got the situation completely under control."

Five minutes later my mother handed me a bag of garbage and asked me to take it outside. I opened the door to the garage, stared down at the steps, and spotted my favorite sneakers, which had been removed from Frankie's feet. I slipped them on and headed out the door.

After running the garbage outside, I reached into a box by the door and picked out the pair of skates Eddie let me borrow. I put on my coat and walked down Broadway Avenue. When I arrived at Eddie's house, I took quiet steps and moved quickly. I gently rested the skates on the porch and turned around to leave.

Then the door creaked open. I turned around and froze. Eddie stepped outside and bent over to pick up the skates.

"I didn't know you were home," I said nervously.

"You could have tried knocking," he replied.

A second of silence passed. "Thanks for letting me use the skates," I muttered. Then I turned to leave.

"Are you still mad about losing?" he asked me.

I stopped and turned back. "Yeah."

"Me, too," he said.

At that point I wished I had knocked on the door and handed him his skates. Even though he got on my nerves on a regular basis, Eddie had helped us. Because of him, we'd actually come close to winning. While I was sure that he'd be back to his old annoying tricks soon, I owed him something. "Thanks for playing on our team," I said.

He stared away from me and shrugged. Then he looked down at the hockey skates in his hand. "You could have kept the skates," he muttered awkwardly.

"Maybe you can lend them to somebody else who needs them," I said.

About the Author

TRIVIA QUESTION: What is Title IX?

If you know the answer, you deserve a high five. If you're not sure, here are a few helpful hints:

1. It's a national law that was passed in 1972.

2. It's otherwise known as: gender equity. (Define each word and put them together.)

3. It has to do with something we have in common.

You can do it! Don't give up!

In book-tour visits to over 100 cities and 250 bookstores, only a handful of kids have known the answer to this question without the hints. When you get the answer, you'll understand why this is such an important question.

Here are explanations of the clues:

1. Gender means male or female.

2. Equity means the state of being just, partial, or fair (equal).

3. Now what do we all have in common? We like sports!

Title IX was passed on June 23, 1972, as part of a

national education act which prohibited gender discrimination in schools and colleges that receive federal funding. Title IX ensures that equal amount of girls get to play sports as boys and vice-versa.

I will never forget the date or age of Title IX because it was passed five days after I was born. If it weren't for this legislation, I would never have had a chance to go to college on a basketball scholarship, write these books, or even play all the sports I did while growing up. Neither would you. Imagine—whether you are a girl or boy—if you were like most of the women of my mother's generation who walked into a gym and were told to leave. What if the only place you could play ball was in your backyard or at the park? Or if you had a sister who worked harder than any kid in the neighborhood and she didn't have a team to play for because she was a girl?

Pop quiz: What is Title IX? Don't look back at the words I've written. Think about it. Tell your friends or somebody at home. Appreciate the opportunities that Title IX has given us and our sisters and cousins. Someday you might have a daughter and will be thankful that she has a fair shot to live her dream.

Whether you become a professional athlete or play at the local gym or park, the strength sports gives boys, girls, men, and women is something that will stay with you forever.

We all deserve a chance to feel strong.

Visit
www.bplayers.com
Broadway Ballplayer World Headquarters

- E-mail your favorite Ballplayer
- Get your own free e-mail account
- Download, print, and share free Ballplayer trading cards
- Send sports e-cards to teammates and friends
- Get sports tips, play games, and chat in the stands and in huddles
- Write to author Maureen Holohan
- Get the scouting report on upcoming books and future Ballplayers
- Click on the link to our teammates at girlslovesports.com